SIREN SONG

No planets I've ever been on are like Damos. Looking, I feel a strange surge of excitement. I decide it must be the challenge. A new world. A new life. No computers. No screens. Real food. Walking around without your hip-weapons. No neons. No teeming millions. Air that hasn't been recycled a thousand times before it hits your lungs. All those wonderful colours. Sharp, vibrant smells of the sea.

The air is like glass. I lift my face and smell the wind. Feel it on my skin. Through my hair. I swear I can hear voices singing to me.

Calling.

It's as if somebody, somewhere, knows I'm here.

But I haven't got a clue who it can be.

Also in the Point SF series:

Virus
Molly Brown

<u>The Obernewtyn Chronicles:</u>
Obernewtyn
The Farseekers
Isobelle Carmody

Random Factor
Jessica Palmer

First Contact
Nigel Robinson

Scatterlings
Isobelle Carmody

Strange Invaders
Stan Nicholls

Year of the Phial
Joe Boyle

Look out for:

Second Nature
Nigel Robinson

Greed Factor
Jessica Palmer

SIREN SONG

Sue Welford

SCHOLASTIC

Scholastic Children's Books,
Commonwealth House, 1–19 New Oxford Street,
London WC1A 1NU, UK
a division of Scholastic Ltd
London ~ New York ~ Toronto ~ Sydney ~ Auckland

Published in the UK by Scholastic Ltd, 1996

Copyright © Sue Welford, 1996

ISBN 0 590 13386 1

Typeset by DP Photosetting, Aylesbury, Bucks.
Printed by Cox & Wyman Ltd, Reading, Berks.

10 9 8 7 6 5 4 3 2 1

nce once I sat upon a promontory,
nd heard a mermaid on a dolphin's back
tering such dulcet and harmonious breath
at the rude seas grew civil at her song
nd certain stars shot madly from their spheres,
 hear the sea maid's music.

A Midsummer Night's Dream
by
William Shakespeare

For Paul,
who made it so

CONTENTS

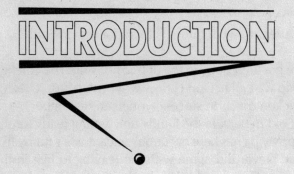

INTRODUCTION

Outbound Voyage

I'm sitting in my cubby trying to decide what to do with my lousy life when my father comes through on the trans-com. It's good to see him. I've kind of missed him since I got my own place.

"Sabra," he says. "Your ma's got a job on Damos. Chief engineer on some marine project – fancy coming?"

Damos? Never heard of the place. But I've travelled all over the universe with my mother so didn't see why now should be any different.

"Sure," I tell my pa. "I'll tag along. Where is Damos anyway?"

"In the eighteenth galaxy," Pa says. "Zone twenty-five. Primitive but peaceful. Still fancy it?"

Sounds OK.

"Why not?" I say.

After all, what future is there for me on Earth?

I've got this cubby in the public housing. The chicken coop we call it. Don't know why. There hasn't been a chicken on Earth since anyone can remember.

So, I'm back in the family unit getting ready for the trip. My pa has kept my cubby vacant. He's funny like that. Never did agree with me leaving to live in the coop. Always said I'd be back one day. But I had to go. I had to be free. Life in the towers was killing me.

All my things are still here. Seeing them makes me feel like a little girl again.

I'm sitting on my bunk, trying to decide what to take. Word has got around we're leaving and the skivvies will be here soon to clean up. I'd hate to get caught in the rush to occupy the space.

My little sister Lu comes and stands by the curtain. She's fourteen, three years younger than me. We're alike. Olive skin, dark green eyes. Same black hair except mine's frizzy and I've never had it cut. Lu's is all done up with some kind of fluorescent green ribbon.

She comes right in and sits on the mattress. She sorts through my things. As usual, she annoys me, touching my stuff.

"Are you taking these?" She holds up a couple of books.

"Yes."

2

I take the books from her. Carefully. They're about a thousand years old. Tales from old-earth legends. Pictures of dragons and mermaids, sea monsters, fairies and kings. Crazy I know but I've loved them all my life.

Lu sighs. "I'm taking all my best clobber. My skin paints. You can't buy that kind of stuff on Damos."

Typical, I think.

"Do we need our translators?" she goes on.

I shake my head. "Pa says most people speak Earther."

"How come?" Lu asks.

I shrug. "Maybe their ancestors were Earth-born. Why ask me? I'm not a walking history-vid."

Lu looks upset. I put my hand on her arm. I try to be nice. After all, she might be my only companion when we get to Damos. Who knows?

"Look Lu," I say gently. "I'm not taking much. Don't believe in lumbering yourself with loads of gear." I put my sketcher, my books, my ancient bear, Sunday, in my sack. Old Sunday's fur's a bit grot but who cares?

"Aren't you taking your skeeter?" Lu asks, cheering up. That's one thing about Lu. She doesn't stay miserable for long.

"What?" I say. "You crazy? As if I'd leave that behind!"

I stroke its shining surface. All the days of my

Summerland childhood are in that sheen. It's had new runners fixed and is in the best condition ever.

They say skeeters mellow with age. Like bears. And people. I suppose.

I say goodbye to all my buddies. Janey. Shark. Studs. Skin. I'll miss Skin more than anyone. We had a thing going once but he wanted to settle down. Have kids. I'm not into all that.

We meet for the last time in the Fun Centre on the city's west four thousand and ninth parallel. It would have been nice to have somewhere quiet to go.

We find a free space on the five hundred and fiftieth floor. As usual the lifts are out. By the time we get up there we're knackered.

The sound of the rain falling from the dome and the screech of the sky-trains make conversation hard. It's not surprising my buddies envy me leaving this hell-hole of a planet.

We sit around the screen. Down a few beers. We talk about old times. The fun we had. Now and then klaxons rip the air. Searches shine through the slits. We keep well down. The last thing I want is to get busted before I leave. I'm clean anyway but they'd never believe me until they'd searched. Some of those male droids can be really rough. I've had bruises to prove it.

We play a few rock-vids. Really ancient some of them. Elvis the King, worn and misty from aeons of time. Others too. Metal favourites from the old zip-gun days. Ones that will remind me of my Earth friends for ever.

They all wish me luck. Skin's eyes glisten with tears. I pretend I haven't noticed.

"I'll send telenews," I say. Then I remember there are no screens on Damos. For a minute I get cold feet. But I've made up my mind to go and that's that.

The ship is vast and slow. One of the biggest I've been on. It's ferrying ore from Callisto to Hecate and will drop us off on the way. It doesn't cater for passengers.

I spend a lot of time skeeting along the kilometres of corridors that flank the cargo bays. Luckily they've got a work-out room. At least I'll manage to keep in shape. If the natives on Damos are hostile I'll need my muscles.

I make friends with some of the crew. I don't get as friendly as my sister though. She's certainly glad of her face paints. They hide the bags under her eyes.

I spend some time on the bridge with the captain. I'd been at school with one of her kids. She shows me the controls. Lets me handle them. She says I'd make a good pilot. It's too late now – there are no training schools on Damos and I've only got a one-way ticket.

I spend time in the video-cab too. I learn about Damos.

It turns out to be a tiny almost-forgotten Earth-type 9

planet. Immigrants from one of Earth's islands settled there about ten generations ago. They'd integrated well with the humanoids already there. The civilization's technologically backward. There's only one big land mass and most of that's been reclaimed from the sea by centuries of drainage. There's a few small groups of volcanic islands, only a few inhabited. Central government's on the Mainland continent. Most of the pioneers settled on Narran, our destination. Narran's one of a small chain of otherwise uninhabited islands smack in the middle of the Perfidian sea. It's practically self-sufficient. Why they should suddenly need an Earther engineer no one knew. My ma is expecting to be briefed on arrival. Anyway, she'd said. A job's a job, isn't it? A chance to escape. Why ask questions?

One trax catches my eye. Shot by the original Seekervessels it shows footage of the wildlife of Narran. Most lives on the Island Heights – low foothills at the base of an extinct volcano in the centre of the island. The rest live in or near the ocean. One trax I play again. A beautiful sea creature. "Thought to be one of the most ancient indigenous species of the planet," the voice-over drones. The creature reminds me of something I've seen before but I can't think what. Where. Then I realize. Pictures in my book of old-Earth legends. Half humanoid, half fish. Sea-Siren. Mermaid... Call it what you like. Seeing it sends shivers down my spine. Don't know why.

I play the trax again. There's something about the Siren. Her movements seem to hypnotize me. The way she swims and dives. The way her hair shimmers green and blue just below the surface of the water. The tail-flick of moon-silver like she's part of the patterns of the ocean.

I play it one more time...

I can see Damos is going to be interesting. You can get sick of high-tech worlds. Damos is different. Somehow a bit scary. Like we're going back in time. Alien planets you can cope with. Ancient-Earth types are really something else.

I'm watching the trax for the third time when a couple of crew come in. They're Nexans. Usual kind. Grey skin, big ears. Arrogant. They eye me curiously.

"What's so interesting?" I ask, ready for trouble.

"Nothing." Their pink eyes slide away.

They sit and watch the screen.

"They say those creatures are almost extinct," one remarks.

I turn. "Why?"

He shrugs massive shoulders. "How should I know?"

"Killed," the other one pipes up.

A strange bolt of pain shoots through my heart. Why should I care about some primitive sea creature?

Weird, but I do.

"Why?" I ask again.

"They feed on the alga." The Nexan looks at me as if I'm stupid.

"On what?"

"Alga," the Nexan goes on. "Some kind of sea-vegetable. The Narranese harvest it and make it into liquor. It's their main industry."

I shrug. All this is news to me.

"So?" I say.

"So – they killed off most of the Sirens. After all, the population is human."

"So?" I say again.

"So . . . humans only care about themselves." The Nexan snorts through his trunk in disgust. "You're one so you must know that."

I shrug. He's right. I think of all the wild creatures that used to live on Earth. Of animals called dolphins and whales that inhabited the oceans. Seals – exterminated because they ate the fish that men said belonged to them. I think of singing-birds that flew free until they were all killed by chemicals, and sleek, amber cats that were hunted to extinction because men prized their fur.

"How come you know so much, clever dick?" I ask. "You been on Damos or something?"

The Nexan shakes his head. "No trade nowadays. Cargo-ships used to stop there but trade dwindled after they stayed neutral during the stellar wars. It's way off the routes anyway. We're only dropping you off as a favour."

"So how come you know so much about the place then?"

"When you spend as long as we do in space you get to know a lot of things."

I turn back to the screen. The Siren's still there. She leaps and dives. Her dance turns the ocean to magic.

"There's some legend about them," the Nexan's saying. "But I can't remember what."

Maybe I'll find out when I get there.

I turn to go. The other Nexan stares.

"What you looking at?" I ask.

"Are all Earther girls like you?" he asks.

I look down at myself. Studded leather. Leggings. Black boots. Nothing out of the ordinary. I toss my hair back. I narrow my eyes at him. "So what if they are?"

He shrugs. His stare slips away. "Only asked," he mutters.

"Tell me how else you protect yourself?" I say, fingering the zips on one of my jackets.

They can't think of an answer so they change the subject, ask me why I'm leaving Earth.

"It's got to be the worst place in the universe," is the answer. "Why else?"

The outbound journey seems to take for ever. My parents opted for a sleep-package. Wish I'd done the same.

When we get off the shuttle, Lu cries. She's in love

with one of the engineers. I'd warned her not to get tangled up. I know about these star-ferry crewmen. She ignored me as usual.

The hatches open and I step out.

There's a few people lined up behind the perimeter fence. One or two are watching through some kind of eyeglass.

I look beyond them to the sea. Take great, deep lungfuls of fresh air.

I think I'll always remember my first sight and smell of Narran. Hills rich with vegetation. Small town leading down to a tiny harbour. White cliffs, turquoise-blue ocean edged with golden sand. Looming above it all is the volcano we swooped over in the shuttle as we headed for the pad.

"Been extinct for centuries," my ma had said, straining her impact harness to get a good look out of the porthole.

No planets I've ever been on are like Damos. Looking, I feel a strange surge of excitement. I decide it must be the challenge. A new world. A new life. No computers. No screens. Real food. Walking around without your hip-weapons. No neons. No teeming millions. Air that hasn't been recycled a thousand times before it hits your lungs. All those wonderful colours. Sharp, vibrant smells of the sea.

It's really weird but in an odd way I feel I'm coming home. Who knows, maybe I am?

Across barren salt flats, the ocean-shore is fringed with trees. Maybe some folk memory stirs?

The air is like glass. I lift my face and smell the wind. Feel it on my skin. Through my hair. I swear I can hear voices singing to me.

Calling.

It's as if somebody, somewhere, knows I'm here.

But I haven't got a clue who it can be.

Damos

We're greeted by some guy called Homer. It turns out he's governor of this island. Appointed by something called the Gummant party in power on Mainland.

Homer looks us up and down. I glare back. Then he smiles irritatingly as if we've passed some kind of test.

He takes us to our unit. His limmo's an old Hondacar. I guess it had been imported from Earth in the days when cargo-liners called here.

Our unit's only on two levels. It takes up so much ground area it almost freaks me out. It's made of wood and looks as if the wind might puff it away. It's near the ocean-shore. No other units in sight. I've got this whole cubby to myself.

A dozen families on Earth could occupy the space. Homer says it's called a cottage.

My bedroom window faces the sea. My vision's filled with the wide, shimmering sand. The sun, a great golden eye. Looking. I open the casement and the dry, ocean winds touch my face with fingers of welcome. I can see the crescents of Damos's twin moons suspended like grey daytime ghosts in the endless, azure sky.

I unpack my gear faster than light. I get my skeeter. I run down the stairs. My ma's gone off with Homer to get her briefing for the project. As they go out I hear him say something about a new offshore distillery.

My pa's putting stuff away in the cooking-room cupboards.

"I'm going out," I tell him.

He looks alarmed. "Be careful, Sabra."

I make a face at him. I suppose I'll have to put up with being told what to do until I find a unit of my own.

Outside, warm air kisses my cheek. I take off my jackets and leggings. Unlace my boots. I keep on my shorts and vest. My leathers are going to be too damned hot here I can see. The trax said the climate was sultry, stormy – a monsoon season in late summer. I'll just have to hope I don't get into any fights.

I stand a minute looking at the sky. It's blue. Wide and clear to the horizon. A solitary white cloud puffs its way slowly across my vision. I take a deep breath. The fresh air almost burns my lungs. I smell the sea.

I smell space. Freedom.

Beyond the gate is a long, yellow stretch of wind-blown sand. No people in sight. A few trees with leaves like birds' feathers, grow sky high. One's bent, misshapen. Its foliage touches the sand. The sun reflects on the waves, edging their tips with gold. There are sky-birds too. Sea-skimmers I guess. They spin and dive overhead, screaming like jet-rockets.

I put my skeeter down and kick the starter. The motor guns. I balance perfectly and skim across the sand as if I was one of those sky-birds. It's great. The best ever. I can feel sand whistling up between my toes. I feel I'm flying free. Up towards the sun, beyond the atmosphere into the star-shot edges of eternity.

Oh, boy ... even Summerland was never like this.

I skim a couple of kilometres then a steep penin-sula cuts the beach in two. I'm curious to see what's up there.

I tuck my board under my arm and climb the rough-hewn flight of steps to the top.

It's Narran – the island town. Looks a real dump. Small dwellings. Red-roofed. Built close together like they're scared of spaces in between. On a hill above the town are a knot of bigger houses. Built close together too. Pollution from some factory rises in the distance. I guess it must be the old distilling plant that turns alga into the famous Narranese liquor. Beyond, the Island Heights rise like the green humps of a Raxan water-dragon. Then, further beyond, almost invisible in a blue haze – the volcano.

Over the tops of the hills, white clouds drift like puffs of smoke from a primitive cannon. They sail gently into the distance as if they have all the time in the world.

Suddenly I understand why most Earthers are scared of open spaces.

You feel small.

Being small on Earth generally means you're dead.

In the harbour I can see the Narranese trawlerboats lined up along the quay. At the end of the breakwater is a statue of some kind. It looks weird, as if it's rising from the sea. I can't make out what it's of.

I tread on a sharp flint. Swearing, I sit to investigate. Suddenly I'm aware someone else is here. My hand flies to my side. No gun. Damn. I'll have to rely on my fists.

He sits on a bank a few metres ahead of me. He's chewing something. He looks about my age. I can see he's taller than me. Dark hair. Tanned skin. His trousers are red. Tight. Definitely sexy. I wonder if all the boys in Narran look like him.

He stands up slowly and comes towards me. I stand up too, hands outstretched so he'll know I'm unarmed. That way I hope to surprise him.

He says something in a language I don't understand.

When I look blank he says it again. This time he speaks Earther.

"Cut your foot?" he asks, grinning.

His eyelashes are very long.

"Not really," I say, wary in case he jumps me.

"Let's have a look."

I back off. "Stay away," I hiss. Automatically I put my hand to my hip and curse again when there's no weapon to reassure me.

"Hey!" he spreads his hands. "Take it easy. Who are you anyway?"

"What's it to you?"

He shrugs again. "Nothing – just curious."

"Where I come from it's dangerous to be curious."

A ghost of a smile crosses his face. "Where's that?" he asks.

"Want to know a lot, don't you?"

"OK. OK. Just trying to be friendly, that's all."

I relax a bit. "I'm from Earth," I tell him. "Where d'you think?"

He raises his eyebrows. They are thick, dark like his hair. "Oh, yeah – I heard a shuttle landed. Quite an event. What you come to Narran for?"

"Why should I tell you?" I ask.

The boy sighs and spreads his hands wide. "I'm just trying to show a polite interest. And stop looking as if you think I'm going to thump you." He grins irritatingly.

16

He's got to be joking. If anyone's going to be doing any thumping it'll be me.

I relax a bit more but still eye him warily. I've met his sort before. Put you at your ease then jump you when you turn your back.

"My ma's got a job here," I say.

"Yeah?" he says. Then he tells me some ancient ancestors of his were Earthers. "Generations ago," he says.

"How interesting," I say sarcastically.

He ignores me. "What kind of job's your ma got?"

I nod my head to indicate the mass of scaffolding where something is being built in the sound between Narran and a couple of rocky islands. "She's an engineer," I tell him. "If that's a distillery being built out there I guess that's where she's working."

He seems impressed. "Yeah, it is. No one knew anything about it until they started," he says. "Caused a bit of trouble with the locals. They're scared they'll lose their jobs when they shut the old one down. It's got a cordon around it a mile wide."

"Yeah?"

"You sure your foot's OK? There's loads of poison thistles around here." He puts his hand out as if he's going to take a look at it. I draw back.

"Sure. I said so, didn't I?"

The boy eyes me shrewdly. "What's your name?"

There doesn't seem to be any harm in telling him. So I do.

"Mine's Troy," he tells me although I haven't
asked.

But he's definitely attractive so I crack a grin and
say, "Hi."

He grins back.

It seems I've made my first friend on Damos.

I'm right about Narran. It is a dump.

I go there with my pa and Lu to suss the place out.
There are a few cafés, bars. Old guys and a few
mangy dogs dozing in the morning sun.

I want to go into one of the bars, try this famous Elix
the Narranese cook up at their smelly old distillery.
My pa refuses. I don't want to leave him and Lu by
themselves so I stay close.

I make up my mind I'll come back later by myself.

Down by the quay is an open market. It's like one I
saw once on Manja 3. Fresh food's laid out. Blue and
pink plants. A black kind of weed my pa says is the
alga harvested by the trawlerboats. Most goes to the
distillery, he explains, but the local housewives like
to cook it as a vegetable. I lift a handful. It's slimy,
smells dark, metallic. I screw up my face. There's
poor dead sea creatures too, eyes, mouths wide open.
They're laid out on stone slabs. They look as if they
died in agony. My stomach churns. The stalls selling
fruit smell of sunshine. Lots of women bustle about
with shopping bags.

"It's going to be tough for you here, Pa," I say, thinking he'll feel out of place.

He shrugs and smiles. "I'll manage," he says.

I leave him and Lu doing the shopping and wander along the breakwater. Ropes cover the sidewalk like snakes. In the trawlerboats men are oiling the huge wheels that pull in the nets. They stare as I walk past.

I stare back.

At the end of the wall is the statue. I can see it's a Siren. Her arms are held out in welcome. Her hair floats behind, its beauty captured in stone. I climb up and gently touch the carved scales of her tail.

I hear my pa calling.

On a corner street-kids loll. I look at them with interest but they only stare back. Hostility shows in their eyes. The girls wear weird clothes. Frocks. Ribbons hang like weeds. Some kind of traditional dress I guess. They look down their noses at me and Lu. I'm really pleased I'm wearing my leathers, even if I am sweating like a ground-pig. I toss my hair from my eyes and look at them defiantly.

Lu nudges me. "They're staring at you, Sabra."

"So?"

"If you smile they'll know you want to be friends."

"Who says I want to be friends?"

My pa butts in.

"You might not actually find the locals too sociable," he says. "There's a bit of resentment here about the new distillery. Nothing to worry about though," he adds, as if I need reassurance.

"Well, I'd like to make friends," Lu says in a pathetic, little-girl voice. She looks up at my pa. "They won't be violent like street-kids on Earth, will they, Pa?"

I almost throw up.

Pa puts his arm round Lu's shoulders. "I don't expect so, Lu. This is a very peaceful place. The people are mostly content." He throws me a warning glance.

The street-kids look anything but content to me.

Lu smiles. She's not like me. Not streetwise. Not wary. She'll have to learn the hard way I suppose.

Troy appears from an alleyway. He says something to the kids. They drift off. One or two glance back at me. Troy turns and raises his hand. I raise mine back.

A few days later I see him again.

It's late evening. Almost night. I plan to explore the town. Maybe call in at the Net and Skimmer for a drink.

I feel happier after dark. More like home.

I go out first to skeet along the sands. It's a gorgeous night. Sunset. Kissing breezes. The high humidity of the day has mellowed. The twin crescent moons of Damos line up like watch-dogs. One has a green-blue aura like the rings of Saturn. It's the kind of night that makes me glad I've come to Damos. The ocean is calm like smooth, dark wine. I need its tranquillity to wash away my Earth-sickness. Sickness that comes from loneliness. From missing my friends.

I skeet for a while, then stop to sit at the edge of the ocean. I listen. It seems to be singing to me. A mournful song. Like the old, sad rock numbers we'd loved so much. Like the song that called to me the day we landed.

And then I see her.

She swims a few yards from the shore. I can hardly believe my eyes. But there's no mistaking.

It's the wild Sea-Siren that lives within my dreams.

Her dark head breaks the surface. Behind, her tail kicks a wave of silver and of gold. She's the same as the one on the vid-trax. More beautiful than any old-Earth legend. More beguiling than the breeze.

She's come to sing to me. I swear it.

I hold my breath, scared to let it out in case it frightens her off. The sound of her voice makes the hair on the back of my neck stand on end. The blood races through my veins like fire. As she sings, her slender, lithe body leaps and dives like a fairy creature. She's the most incredibly beautiful thing I've ever seen. It seems she's sending thoughts to me across the waves the way the legends say they can. I feel all the fantasies of my childhood coming true.

I know now why the trax fascinated me. Why I wanted more than anything to see a Sea-Siren for real. I know she heard my heart call out.

I sit there and watch.

Spellbound.

Starstruck.

Seduced.

I know I've been chosen. I know she's there for me alone. Her voice sings its wild and beautiful song. The song that rides the wind like a sky-bird.

Slowly I get to my feet. She's drawing me towards her with an enchanted thread. The air is full of melody. It seems to envelop and absorb the very night itself. Her song is of blue skies, emerald oceans. Of deep sea caves and spires of beauty and jewels. Of restful, safe havens. Things I thought only existed in the history of man's imagination. She haunts me, calms me. All the uncertainty, the violence of my life on the streets of Earth; all my heartbreak at leaving my friends are nothing but one single beat of my lonely heart.

All I want is to be near to her. To feel her magic touch me.

I walk into the water.

But then I see something else. Another sinuous, dark shape. It swims towards the Siren. I think at first it's another one and that I'll get to see a love-dance. I've got a weird feeling a Siren love-dance shouldn't be seen by anyone.

But it isn't another one. It's something else. A black, sinister creature. It speeds towards her. Its fin cuts the water like a Samuran dagger-blade. The singing stops, then there's this terrible, screaming silence. The Siren thrashes wildly and all at once the sea is foaming red. I yell and plunge in deeper. My hand reaches automatically, hopelessly, for my gun.

Behind, I hear a shout. Splashing. Someone grabs me. I yell. I struggle and swear but it's no good. The Siren's gone. Disappeared for ever in a wash of scarlet.

The black shape slides away.

I can hear something else.

Someone wildly screaming.

I guess it must be me.

I'm kicking out. I shout. I feel tears on my face. I haven't cried since I was a kid.

"Sabra, Sabra!" a voice says through my hair.

It's Troy.

I let him drag me from the water. My grief must have made me weak. I wrench away. I wipe my face on the sleeves of my jackets. I feel studs scratch my cheek.

"Leave me alone!" I yell. I turn my back so he won't see the tears.

He takes hold of me again. "I had to get you away," he shouts. "The swark would have killed you too."

"I can look after myself!" I shake him off. I grab my skeeter and walk away down the beach. My hair falls over my face. It's like a shroud of mourning. I feel as if part of me has been taken away.

Troy runs after me.

"Didn't anyone warn you swarks sometimes come to these waters?"

"That to the swarks!" I gesture with my fingers.

Troy grabs my arm. "Sabra, what were you doing anyway, going into the water like that – especially at night? You loony or something?"

I turn to face him. I know my eyes are blazing. "I do what I damned well like!"

Troy shrugs. "Get yourself killed if you want to. It's no skin off my nose."

He walks away.

Now it's my turn to run.

"Troy!"

He turns. His face looks angry, hurt. His eyes blaze back at me. "What?"

"Did you see her?"

"Who?"

"The Siren."

In the moons-light his hair is the colour of jet.

I walk along beside him. My hand brushes his. I think about taking hold of it. I'm glad he's here. Talking might ease my pain and help me forget. I've lived with violence all my life but seeing that creature killed has cut me to bits. This treacherous planet's no better than anywhere else.

Troy doesn't answer when I ask him if he's seen the Siren.

I ask him again.

He picks up a bit of driftwood and flings it into the sea. Then he stops walking and sits down. He draws his knees up to his chin. His face is serious in the moons-light.

I sit beside him. My shoulder touches his.

"Yes," he says at last. "I saw her. She used to swim near here a lot." His voice is full of sadness.

"You've seen her before then?"

"Yep."

"I felt..."

"What?"

"I felt she was singing just for me."

Troy looks at me. He frowns. "Maybe she was."

"Is it true they're nearly extinct?"

"So they say." Troy drags his eyes from my face and stares out across the water. "My grandfather Skipperjon says there were quite a few around when he was a youngster. They used to gather on the rocks under Narran Point."

"Didn't anyone try to stop them being killed?"

Troy shrugs. "A few people I guess. But the trawlermen had to make a living... You know what it's like. They thought harvesting alga would make them rich. As it is," he says bitterly, "it's the Gummant bigwigs that are making all the money."

I put my hand on his arm. His sweatshirt's soaked. "Someone said there was a legend..."

Troy looks at me again. He puts his hand towards my face. I draw back quickly then realize he means no harm. He waits until I relax, then tucks my hair behind my ear.

I feel like kissing him.

"What legend's that?" he asks.

I shrug. "I dunno. Some Nexan said there was a legend about the Sirens."

"There's one about the ocean goddess, Sirena. I learned it at school. One of the few things I did learn..."

"Tell me that one then."

"I wouldn't have thought someone like you would have cared about old fairy stories."

"Try me," I say.

Troy lays back on the sand, his face to the moons. I draw my knees up to my chin and stare out to the horizon.

"Once," he goes, "when Chrysos, the golden god-king of Damos was riding the skies in his coral chariot, he saw the beautiful maiden Luna and desired her. He took her for his wife. But Luna was wicked and greedy. She wanted Chrysos' kingdom of Damos for herself. So she raised a great storm. The seas rose and overwhelmed the land. But, unbeknown to Luna, Chrysos had been taken to a place of safety by the ocean goddess, Sirena, and when the waters receded, Chrysos banished Luna to live in the sky. She was destined for ever to encircle Damos in tandem with the goddess Ananke. You can still see her on a clear night..." Troy points upwards. I lie back and stare at the sky. "...You can see the millions of tiny asteroids that orbit Luna. They're supposed to be her tears of regret. The legend says if any of these fall to the earth a great disaster will overwhelm the land."

When I don't say anything Troy sits up. "Well..." he says, staring at me. "You asked me to tell you..."

"What's it all supposed to mean?" I ask, puzzled.

"It doesn't mean anything. It's just a legend. Even Earthers have legends, don't they?"

"They used to," I say. Then, "Where did the legend of Chrysos and Luna come from?"

He shrugs. "Dunno, just handed down from generation to generation I suppose."

I suddenly remember the statue in the harbour. "Why is there a statue of a Siren at the harbour entrance?" I ask.

Troy shrugs again. "Dunno," he says. "Something to do with the old religion I suppose."

"What old religion?"

"One people used to practise – in the olden days. No one bothers now."

I think about what he's said. About the legend of the goddess Sirena. About my beautiful Siren whose death has broken my heart.

"You know, Troy," I say, "she was singing just for me. I felt it in my mind."

"Yeah," he says. "Some people can. That's why they're afraid of them."

"Who's afraid of them?"

I'm surprised. How can anyone be scared of a creature like that? They should go to Centurai if they want to see something to be scared of.

"Some people just are," Troy says.

"Not you though."

"No." Troy picks up a piece of dried sea-vegetable and cracks it between his fingernails. "Not me." He lets the fragments crumble through his fingers on to the sand.

I run my hands through my hair. It's beginning to dry and is stiff with sea salt. "Why not?" I ask, looking at him sideways.

"Something happened to me," Troy explains. "When I was a kid..."

I wait for him to go on. When he doesn't I touch his arm again. "What...?"

He looks down at my fingers resting on his sleeve. I snatch my hand back. I don't want to put him off.

"I don't really remember all of it ... I was only about four years old... I fell off my grandfather's boat in Selkie Sound..."

"Yeah," I say. "So...?"

Troy shakes his head. "I don't know why I'm telling you this. I've never talked about it before..."

"You haven't told me anything yet."

"No." There's silence for a minute then Troy goes on. "Everyone thought I'd drowned," he says. "I remember falling in, thrashing about, then going down under the water. Everything was green and blue and there were weird noises. Like some kind of music. I was really scared..."

"Yeah? What of?"

"Of drowning, stupid... Swarks, anything..."

He's taking a chance calling me stupid but I let it pass.

"Yeah ... OK ... OK ... go on."

"Then ... nothing really. Except ... there seemed to be figures all around me. Helping me. Telling me everything was going to be OK. I ... I don't know really. The next thing I knew I was lying on the beach near the wharf and later a search party coming with flares to find me. I tried to tell them but they just thought I'd gone a bit loony, swallowing sea water and stuff..." Troy breaks off as if he's lost in a maze of words.

"Do you think it was a Siren saved you?"

"I don't know. If it was, then no one would've believed me. I was only a kid. In the end they convinced me I'd been dreaming."

"But you're not sure."

Troy looks out at the sea again. "No," he says. "I've never been sure."

Troy gets up and holds out his hand for me. I ignore it and get to my feet.

"You're shivering," he says. "You'd better get back."

"I'm OK. A midnight swim won't do me any harm." I manage a grin. "Shall I walk you home?"

Troy shakes his head. He smiles, "I was going to say that to you."

I raise my eyebrows. "It's OK. I can look after myself."

Troy looks at me as if he doesn't believe me.

"Is that where you live?" he says, pointing to the cottage along the dunes.

"Uh-huh."

"Some guy from Earth lived in that place years ago."

"Yeah?"

"My grandad knew him – bit of a weirdo. Apparently, he lived by the sea on Earth or something."

I crack another grin. "By the sea? On Earth? You've got to be joking. It's so full of garbage the fumes would kill you."

Troy walks a few hundred metres along the shore with me. At the bottom of the steps he stops. "What is that?" he asks, pointing to my skeeter board.

I tell him.

"Don't come here again at night, Sab," he warns before we part. "It's really dangerous."

"I thought everyone here was supposed to be free to do what they want."

"Well," he says with a shrug. "It's your neck."

I watch him run up the steps. At the top he turns but doesn't wave.

I make my way slowly home. I vow I'll come to the beach every night in case another Siren comes.

Suddenly, as I stroll back, the wind gets up. It catches my hair and blows it across my face. Great breakers pound the shore. My hair is whipped into madness. Darkening clouds whizz across the moons. I can feel the ocean spray stinging my face and when I lick my lips the salt is like blood.

At home I lie and listen to the storm wheezing and groaning outside. The house feels like it's going to blow. Rain lashes the eaves. For some stupid reason I feel scared. There's something about this place I can't make out. I suppose it's because I'm used to the consistent weather on Earth. The eternal dampness of the domes. At least you know what to expect.

I put my head under the pillow and cradle old Sunday in my arms.

Eventually I sleep.

When I awake I can still hear great breakers pounding the shore. Shivering, I get out of bed and look through the window. The wind has dropped. Luna and Ananke, swarms of bright stars, decorate the sky. The sea still looks angry.

I listen.

No Siren songs drift across the waves.

No melody comes to haunt my dreams for ever.

At Lyxa's

A couple of nights later I find myself back in Narran. I've been skeeting along the shore. The storm has thrown up all kinds of rubbish and the run's been really hard.

In the Net and Skimmer a bunch of street-kids sit in the corner. Troy's with them. And my sister Lu. As I go in Troy raises his hand and grins at me.

A couple of men sit by the door. They wear jackets with the name of my ma's company on. No one's talking to them.

The bar's crowded. Smoke hangs in the air like ghosts. The place stinks. It reminds me of Earth.

I find a stool at the bar. The barman dumps a mug of Elix in front of me with a grunt. It tastes like garbage. I order a beer. At the far end of the room, next to the sign that says "lavatory", the juke thumps out some heavy stuff. I glance over my shoulder. Troy's speaking to some pale youth in a red cap. Beside me, two trawlermen are talking about the annual carnival due this month. They're laughing about something they saw last year.

One turns to look at me. He says something in Damosian to his companion.

Another man pushes in beside me and orders beer. He drinks it all in one go. He wipes his mouth on his sleeve, then looks at me.

"You're the girl from Earth." It's not a question so I don't answer. I take a swig of my beer and look him up and down. "Some kind of warrior or something they tell me," he goes on.

I wonder if he's trying to be funny.

"I've seen you on that." He indicates my board tucked under the stool. "Do all Earthers have them?"

I smile, deciding there's no harm in being friendly. "Only the lucky ones who get to go to Summerland."

"Summerland?"

It's obvious he's never been to the place so I tell him about the asteroid. He pulls a face as if he thinks I'm making it up.

He orders another beer. "I've heard things about Earth-girls," he says slyly, when he's knocked it back in one go.

He has that look in his eye I've seen a million times.

I raise my eyebrows and try to keep cool. "Yeah?"

He pokes one of the studs on my jacket. "Especially you street-kids. I bet you're pretty free and easy, aren't you?"

I manage to crack a grin. "Don't believe everything you hear."

Really, I feel like punching his greasy face in. I resist the temptation. I don't know why. I've met jerks like him all over the galaxy and it's the only kind of language they understand. And anyway, ever since I saw that Siren killed I've been dying to punch someone.

I decide to ignore him so I turn my back and lean my elbows on the bar. Then I feel the trawlerman's hand on my leg. It's clear he doesn't have a clue I'm a diamond belt and could kill him with one chop.

"How about coming outside with me?" he goes.

I turn around and put my foot on the front of his stool. I see him freeze.

"How about you going to hell?" I say.

I can see the sweat on his face. I can smell the sharp, dark smell of alga on his skin.

I draw back my leg to push but he wriggles backwards off the stool. He stands up. He grins bravely. "Think you're tough, don't you?"

"Don't you then?" I ask.

From the corner of my eye I see one of the girls get up from the corner. She comes past. She looks at me but doesn't smile. She goes through the door by the juke. As she opens it I get a glimpse of a narrow back-alley littered with garbage.

The trawlerman follows her out.

I take another swig of beer. I feel depressed. In the mirror I see couples getting up to dance. Someone puts an old Elvis the King number on the box. It's good to hear it but it really finishes me off. I am lonesome tonight and there's no place for me to go but home.

I get up. I glance towards the kids in the corner. They sit with their heads together, laughing. I think about going over, asking Lu if she's coming with me. I decide against it.

I need the bathroom so I go out the back. The alley stinks. In the distance a bandog howls. Piles of garbage have been spilled from a bin. Rotting food. Elix bottles. Greasy paper. Excrement. A grey scav with long silver tails runs out from under a box.

My stomach churns.

I prop my board up against the door and go in.

I'm just about to come out when I hear a scuffle from the other side of the door. A noise like someone's choking. A muffled cry. I wrench open the door and lurch outside.

Behind a pile of boxes I see two figures struggling. I go round to get a better view. My friend from the bar's got the girl in a death-lock. One hand grips her waist, the other's over her mouth. She's struggling. I see her eyes. Wide. Frightened. Pleading.

He's so intent on his business that he doesn't hear me. He's taller than me but I reach up and get hold of his hair. I pull back as hard as I can. He swears and lets go of the girl. He turns, lashes out. I dodge but his fist thumps my arm. I kick him as hard as I can. He grunts, doubles up. He falls down in the filth of the alley. His face is buried in a pile of rotting summer-fruit.

I take my knife from my belt, squat down and nick a piece from his ear. He screams. The blood runs. The scar will remind him of me. He struggles to his feet, one hand pressed over his ear. He stands there, breathing hard. I see the red light of fury in his eyes. So I turn as if I'm leaving, then send him a high dwit yop chagi fit to bust his skull. I don't even bother to look at the damage.

I hear the girl running away. Her high heels click on the cobblestones.

I wipe my knife on my vest, pick up my skeeter board and head for home.

Along the shore I take my boots off and let my toes sink into the sand. Out to sea the trawlerboats chug back to harbour. Their lights string pearls and rubies against the sky. The framework of the new distillery looks stark and black. It's a really weird design. When Ma comes home I'll ask if I can go out there. Maybe she'll get me a crew job. I can't waste my life waiting for the Siren to return.

Tonight my dreams are full of Siren songs. They try to tell me something but I don't know what. For some strange reason Troy's there too. He's coming round the harbour wall in a red and blue sailing dinghy. His body is lean, brown. There are two wild and beautiful creatures dancing, weaving in his wake.

Old legends say dreams foretell the future. It's probably a load of crap but there are stranger things in the universe than that.

Next day I'm in the town library. I'm curious about this island. Its legends. Its history.

I've spent the morning sitting on the shore reading my Earth-books. My pa's gone shopping and Lu's off with some guy she's met. My arm is black and blue.

The sun is turning my skin golden. I've tied my hair up on top with ribbons I pinched from my sister's box. The breeze on the back of my neck feels wonderful.

At the library there's a man behind the desk. He looks at me over the rim of his glasses as if I've crawled from the woodwork.

"Ticket?" he says.

I don't know what the hell he's on about.

"I just want to look at some history books."

"Do you want to take them out?"

I shrug. "Not really."

"Well if you do, you need to join."

I've no intention of joining. I'm definitely not the joining type.

A girl comes over. I've seen her before. She wears the traditional Damosian dress. A frock, white with flowers on. I've seen flowers growing on the hill. Real ones with colours brighter than a Martian sunset. She wears little sandals, her toes peep through the ends. On each finger she wears a ring.

She smiles. "Can I help?"

"Show this ... er ... person the history section," the deskman goes.

"I really want myths and legends," I tell the girl as I follow her down the aisle between shelves. Then I say, "Please." I just remembered Pa said good manners are important here.

The girl takes me to a section by the stairs. She points out a few volumes.

"These might be what you want. The history section's round the other side. I'm afraid we don't have a great selection. Not much demand, you see." She smiles at me sweetly.

"Thanks," I say, grinning.

I get lost in those books. They tell me more about Narran than any vid-trax. You can read a civilization by its legends. There's a chapter telling the folk myths. The caption says they're from old documents housed in a museum on Mainland. The writing's like Venusian script. Other pictures show wall paintings. Wild creatures. Sea monsters and storms. Sail-boats tossed on swelling seas. Mermaids. There's one of a planet in a midnight sky, its moon a silver orb. They

38

were on the walls of an old Narranese temple. It had been knocked down years ago to widen the cobbled street so that bigger wagons could carry the alga up to the distillery. All that had survived of the old building was the statue now standing at the harbour entrance.

When I've finished I grab a few history books. They don't tell me much. Speculation about the ancient civilization that lived in the lower foothills. From stone carvings it looks like they were a farming community, hunting and fishing. Growing and gathering the crops they needed to live. There's pictures of them cutting some kind of vegetable. Carvings of the sun and moon. There seems to be a gap then because the next thing the books document is the emergence of the seashore based community. There's a chapter about the Earther pioneers. Seems they came from one of Earth's islands and wanted to find a similar place to live on Damos. Looks like they taught the Narranese how to harvest the alga and turn it into Elix. Some old recipe handed down from old-Earthers. Then the island was taken over by the central authority on Mainland. I try to find some record of the Narranese objecting, some uprising or other, but there isn't one. I guess Pa must have been right when he said they were a peaceful people. Then there's the emergence of the ruling Gummant party. I turn back to see if I can find the missing bits but it looks like there aren't any.

There's pictures of the sky-port when freighters

used to bring in stuff from Earth before the stellar wars. There's a photo of the first wedding between a Narranese and a female Earther. She's wearing a frock.

Above my head the clock tick-tocks the hours away. The rumbling of my stomach tells me I should eat. I'm hot so I take off my jackets and hang them on the chair. I lean back and put my boots on the table. The guy at the desk clicks his tongue but I ignore him. You've got to be comfortable.

I'm just sitting, daydreaming, trying to work out some kind of answers to my questions when a voice makes me jump.

"You asleep?"

I toss the hair from my eyes. It's Troy.

He's got his sexy red trousers on. They're made of some kind of shiny material. I want to touch them.

Troy pulls up a chair beside me. It makes a loud squeak on the wooden floor. The clerk tuts again. I make a sign at him with my fingers.

Troy grins. "You're beginning to look like a native," he says, touching the flesh of my arm lightly with his fingertips. He draws back when he sees the bruise. He looks at me but says nothing. He picks up the book on myths and legends. "Been trying to find out more about the Sirens?"

"Some," I say. "And the history of Damos but it's a bit sketchy."

Troy shrugs. "Never could get into history... Never could get into anything much."

"Maybe we could go look at that old town some-time."

"Sure. Whenever you like." Then Troy says, "I've been looking for you all day."

"What for?"

"Someone wants to see you."

My warning system rings alarm bells.

"Who?" I ask cautiously.

Troy grins. "Relax Sab, take it easy. Lyxa's mother..."

I frown, not understanding.

"Never heard of any Lyxa, let alone her ma."

"If you'd bothered to stop and find out you'd know the girl you rescued from that creep last night was Homer's daughter."

I raise my eyebrows, surprised he knows. "Who told you about that?"

He shrugs. "Word gets around."

"Well ... so what if she is Homer's daughter. Makes no difference to me."

"So her old lady wants to see you."

"What for?"

"To thank you I guess."

"I'm busy," I say. I've got better things to do than go visiting some crummy governor's house.

Troy looks confused. "Sab, you should come. Her father is the governor."

"I know," I say. "So what?"

"Sab . . . you don't understand."

I take my feet off the desk and sit forward. "What I understand is that if some crummy governor summons you, you go. Right?"

"Right."

I sit back again and put my feet up. "I said I'm busy. I might go later if I can spare the time."

"Sab . . . it's really the governor's *wife* who wants to see you. Homer's out inspecting the new distillery."

I sigh. "OK, OK, as it's his wife I'll go, but normally I wouldn't budge an inch for any governor, right?"

I see that ghost of a smile cross Troy's face. "Right," he says. He makes a mock salute. "Sir!"

I punch his arm. I put on my jackets, pick up the books and take them across to the girl.

"Thanks."

She smiles at me. "Hope to see you again."

"Me too."

Something in her eyes tells me we could be friends.

On our way out I wink at the clerk. His face flames and he looks away.

"Who's the girl?" I ask Troy when we're outside.

"Her name's Ringo."

"I've seen her before."

"In the Net and Skimmer I bet."

Then I remember that she was with the gang of kids.

Propped up against the light-post is Troy's pedal

byke. We walk together along the street. His arm brushes mine.

Troy points out places as we go along. The council office, his old school. The town hall. Stores. One or two battered, rusting groundmotors are parked by the kerb.

"Only a few folk can afford them," Troy explains. "Directors of the distillery mostly. There's only one shipment of gas every month so you can guess who gets it."

"Who needs 'em anyway," I say. "They only pollute the atmosphere."

I ask Troy if I can try out his byke. He laughs when I fall off. I'm so mad I soon get the hang of it. I whizz round in a circle and screech to a halt beside him. A cloud of dust hits his legs.

"Hey, cut it out," he says, brushing dirt off his sexy red trousers.

He runs beside me all the way up the hill to Lyxa's place.

Lyxa's house is built alongside the other posh places at the top of the hill. It's two-storied, white.

"Who lives in the others?" I ask.

"Company directors mostly. Who do you think?"

I look at him because his voice sounds bitter. He's frowning.

Big gates bar our entrance. Troy speaks through some kind of primitive intercom.

The gates swing open and we go in.

Troy parks his byke by some sheds. The doors are open and I see piles of wooden boxes inside.

We go up to the front door.

I'm hot so I take off my jackets again. I sling them over my shoulder. My vest's got a hole in it but I don't care so why should anybody else?

Troy pulls a rope and a bell echoes inside. The door opens and Lyxa's standing there.

"Hi." She stands back and we go in.

I look around. We're in a hall big enough for a dozen earth-units. I think how I'd get killed in the rush when people heard the space was vacant. Some kind of white statue sits on a pedestal. It would look like a Siren if it had a tail.

Pink flowers droop in pots. The walls are painted as blue as the sky.

I whistle.

Through a door I can see a room with lots of books round the walls. There's a drawing board like an antique one my ma used to own. Documents are rolled up on a table.

"Lyxa," Troy says. "This is Sabra."

"We've met," I say. I hold out my hand but Lyxa doesn't seem to know she should shake it. "You OK?"

Lyxa smiles. She looks a bit shy. She looks different from last night. Could be the bruises on her jaw.

She puts her hand on my arm. I pull away. Then

relax. It's crazy to think anyone like her could be a threat.

"I'm fine. Thanks to you." She eyes my arm. "Did that creep give you that bruise? I'm sorry."

I shrug. "It's nothing. Some girls on Earth wear bruises like medals."

Lyxa looks a bit bemused. "Come through," she says. "My mother's in the sitting room."

We go into this big room. Wide, white windows frame a green garden. A pet cat snores on the rug.

This woman stands up and smiles. Then confusion shows in her eyes and the smile wobbles. She wears the reddest lip-paint I've ever seen. I bet Lu'd give her right arm to get hold of some. She comes towards me.

"Mummy," Lyxa pipes up. "This is Sabra."

"But. . .?" She looks more confused than ever.

"You wanted to thank her . . . for last night."

Lyxa's ma waves her hand in the air. "Yes, yes. . . I know, but I thought. . ."

"What did you think, Mrs H.?" I go.

"I thought you were . . . a boy. They just said 'Sabra'. . . When they said you used some kind of self-defence tactics I naturally thought. . . " She breaks off.

There's a kind of embarrassed silence. Then Lyxa's ma comes forward. She hugs me impulsively. Her body smells of flowers. "It doesn't matter anyway. I'm so grateful to you for saving Lyxa from . . . from goodness knows what."

I think we both know what I saved her from but neither of us says it.

"She wants to be careful," I say instead. "Learn some moves."

"Moves?"

"Yeah. A good dwit yop chagi in the ribs and she wouldn't have needed me. You know there's always scum like that around. A girl needs to know how to defend herself."

"Yes ... well... She shouldn't have been in that low-class bar anyway but that's another story. We haven't told her father, of course. I don't know what he'd do if he found out. Actually..." she goes on, "I'd be grateful if you didn't mention it to anyone else. Sit down, er ... Sabra, we'll have some tea."

"You should get that guy arrested," I say, putting my feet up. "He'll just go on attacking women if everyone's afraid to report him."

Mrs H. looks scared. "Oh ... no, we couldn't stand that kind of publicity. It would get in the newsmags... The Gummant wouldn't look too kindly on one of their official's daughters being involved in something like that ... oh, no..." She looks flustered and frightened to death.

"Hopefully he's been punished enough," Lyxa says.

I sigh and sling my jackets on the carpet. What a crazy society where women don't want their attackers punished.

Lyxa disappears, then comes back with a tray. We drink hot brew out of tiny cups. There's little yellow biscuits to eat. They taste sweet ... of summer. Like nothing I ever tasted before. When I ask what they're made of Mrs H. tells me she bakes them with honey.

Then she asks *me* questions.

"What does your father do, Sabra?"

"He's a home-husband," I tell her.

"Sorry?"

"He cooks – stuff like that."

"Professionally?" she asks, frowning.

I don't know what she's on about.

"Sab's mother's working on the offshore distillery," Troy butts in quickly.

Mrs H.'s eyebrows go up. "Oh, that's interesting. Come to think of it my husband did tell me there was an engineer coming from Earth. I naturally thought it was a ... er ... my husband helped design it, did you realize that, Sabra?"

I nod. "Knew he was something to do with it. Why's it being built out at sea? Any idea?"

Mrs H. looks cagey. Then she says. "Er ... something to do with it being easier to offload the alga, then load it straight into cargo boats when it's been distilled and bottled..."

"Sounds logical," I comment.

"The trouble is, you see," Mrs H. goes on, "the harbour here is rather antiquated and so small. The new cargo-ships just can't get into it safely. It was originally my husband's idea you know, to build the distillery offshore.''

"Yes, yes, Mummy," Lyxa mumbles, "so you keep telling everybody."

"Lyxa – you know I'm proud of your daddy. He's such an important man. What with his expertise as a draughtsman and his duties as governor..."

"Yes, yes, Mother," Lyxa says, "you've told me a million times before."

Lyxa's ma looks annoyed.

Embarrassed, we finish the brew and biscuits.

Then Mrs H. stands up and I guess it's time to go.

"Well, Sabra dear, thank you again for being so brave. I'm sorry you were hurt too."

"Think nothing of it, Mrs H.," I say, getting up.

Mrs H. brushes the place where my boots were on the chair.

Lyxa hands me my jackets. "They're very light," she comments. "Are they real leather?"

I chuckle. "You're joking! There's been no real stuff on Earth since anyone can remember."

"Oh?" Mrs H. blinks.

She comes with us to the door. She kisses my cheek. "Come to see us again, Sabra," she says, although I get the feeling she doesn't really mean it. You've only got to look at people's eyes to know they don't mean what they say. "I'd love to hear some stories about Earth."

"Yeah?" I say, thinking she'd really hate to hear

them. That's the trouble with these remote planets. Their inhabitants are so out of touch.

My ma's at home when I get back. She's sitting with Lu at the cooking-room table. I haven't seen her since we landed.

I run in and hug her close. There are lines on her face that weren't there before. She looks tired.

"You OK, Ma?" I say, frowning.

"Yes, don't I look it?" Her voice sounds strange. She's lying. I know it.

"No, not really."

She hugs me again. "Just working too hard, I expect."

I don't press her. She'll tell me when she's ready.

Pa serves us a meal of dead sea-fish and alga. Lu tucks in but I push the stuff around my plate.

"She doesn't eat hardly anything," he tells Ma.

She leans forward and touches my hair. "Sabra – your father works so hard to prepare nice meals. You should really eat them you know."

I shake my head. "I can't eat this stuff. I've tried. It makes me want to throw up."

"That's nice," Pa says. I can tell he's hurt.

"I'm sorry, Pa." I push my plate away and take a tree-apple from the bowl in the middle of the table. Pa sighs. My parents exchange glances. They're probably thinking it's been a mistake for me to tag along. That I've been away from the family unit too long.

Maybe they're right.

"Aren't you happy here, Sabra?" my mother asks.

I shrug my shoulders. It's no good lying to my ma. Never was. "I miss my friends," I say, staring down at my plate.

"You'll make new ones."

"Sure." Then I tell her about Troy and Lyxa. And Ringo.

"I know them too," Lu butts in, her mouth full of food.

I tell them about going to Lyxa's place.

"You've been to the governor's house?" Pa sounds impressed. He's more interested in that than me saving Lyxa's honour. Even Lu stops eating to listen. I tell them Mrs H. thought I was a boy.

They laugh.

"Ma," I say. "Could you get me a job out there? I'm dying of boredom."

Strangely her face closes up. "No," she says quickly. Too quickly.

"Why the hell not?"

"Sabra, it's all men."

I laugh. "So? Think I can't handle it?"

Ma sighs. "Of course you could handle it, Sabra but there's just no vacancies I'm afraid. Anyway ... I might..."

I wait for her to go on. She doesn't.

"You might what?"

Ma's eyes slide away from mine. "I was just going to say I might not complete the job. It's not exactly what I'd had in mind. I suppose it's my own fault for not insisting on getting briefed before we left Earth."

"Ma – you don't mean we're going back!" Lu pipes up. "We can't," she wails. "I like it here ... Ma..."

Ma pats her arm. "No, Lu, I don't suppose it'll come to that." She shrugs. "Maybe things will work themselves out ... We'll see."

I can't make out why she's being so cagey.

I finish my tree-apple. It tastes good. Sweet. The smell reminds me of Summerland. The juice runs down my chin and on to the table. Pa tuts and gets a cloth to wipe it.

Later Ma comes to my room. I'm lying on my bed listening to my rock tapes. I've got my sketcher out, drawing a picture of Narran. Sunday sits next to me. When I hear someone coming I chuck him on to the floor.

Ma comes in and sits on the bed beside me. Her body is lean, bronzed from the sun. Her hair is cut really short. I love her more than anyone in the galaxy.

She puts her hand on my leg.

"We're a bit worried about you, Sab," she says, looking straight at me. I'm worried about her too but I don't say anything.

"Yeah?" I say instead. "Why's that?"

"Well ... hanging around those bars. Why don't you try going to college – there's a good one on Mainland I believe."

"Oh, Ma ... I finished school."

"I know, but study something new."

"Ma, they can't teach me anything I don't already know now, can they?"

Ma shakes her head. I'm right and she knows it.

"Lu's going," she says.

"I'm not like Lu. I have to be out. Free. You know that."

Ma sighs and strokes my hair. "Yes, I do know. I was a lot like you, Sabra."

"What made you do it, Ma?"

For a minute she looks startled. Then she relaxes and smiles. "Do what?"

"Shack up with Pa, have us kids?"

"Believe it or not I fell in love. And it was what your father wanted. I did it for him."

I smile. "Maybe I should have shacked up with Skin."

Ma shakes her head. "I don't think so, Sab. You're too restless." She sighs again. "I don't know what's best for you, Sabra. I really don't."

"Ma, maybe a job would be best for me."

Her face closes up. "No, Sab. Not out there, anyway."

"Why are you so against it?"

She gets up and goes to look out the window. She gazes out over the restless ocean. Even from here I can hear the thump of the surf and the wild skimmer cries echoing over the waves.

Not turning, Ma says, "I can't tell you, Sab – not yet."

"Why not?"

When she does turn her face is hard and angry. I've never seen her look like that before. "Just forget it, Sabra, will you. And don't say any more to your father. I don't want him to worry. You'll just have to trust me that's all."

"Whatever you say, Ma."

I'd trust my mother with my life. We have a great relationship. And I intend to keep it that way so, just for once, I decide to keep my mouth shut.

I'm just about to tell her my theories about Narran and the Sirens when she comes over and gives me a hug.

"I've got to be going, Sab. I promised your father we'd have an early night. I'll see you next time I'm home."

When she's gone I pick up old Sunday off the floor. I hold him close. On my sketcher I've drawn the picture of the planet and its moon I found in the history book. Something's really bugging me but I can't figure out what.

Next door I hear the murmuring voices of my parents. I wonder if they're talking about me. I think about Skin and how we used to lie in my cubby and tell each other our secrets in the one quiet hour before dawn. I remember how the neon flashes outside used to make patterns across his face.

Suddenly a great knot of loneliness ties itself in my stomach. I get up and look out my window. The twin moons of Damos reflect in the sea like searches. I put on my jackets and leggings. I creep downstairs.

Barefoot, I walk along the sand. The breeze kisses my face. The fronds of the feather trees wave like welcoming arms. But no Siren song echoes through the night.

No melody drifts across the waves to ease my loneliness for ever.

On the Heights

Next evening I go to the sky-port. The carnival ship's due and I don't want to miss it.

It's really creepy on the salt-flats at twilight. Floods from the port illuminate the land for kilometres around. The wind rattles the fences and screams through the dry thistlepods like a demented rock band. The red homing beacons glow like a string of rubies.

Quite a few folk have come to watch. Some hold their kids up high to get a good look. Probably the first star-ship the children have ever seen. By the way the pad's cracking up with age it could be the last. Troy said the carnival comes once a year towards the end of summer. Has done ever since he was a kid.

I put my skeeter down and use it as a seat. Over by

the perimeter fence someone's lit a fire. A crowd gather for warmth. I recognize one or two. Ringo from the library. Lyxa. My sister Lu.

I sit quietly. Watching.

The kids call out to each other, kick stones around. One has a bottle of Elix and they pass it around. I think about the time I used to meet my buddies in the bomb-zone. We lit fires, fooled around. Pretended we were warriors and stuff.

But those times are gone for ever and it's stupid to keep thinking about them.

I hunch up with my arms around my knees. Then I feel a hand on my shoulder. I jump up, putting my hand to my belt. It's only Troy. He grins.

"Waiting for the ship?"

"Uh-huh."

"I'd have thought you'd have seen plenty."

I shrug. "It's something to do."

"Come over with us."

"OK."

Troy bends and picks up my board. I try to snatch it back.

"Give me!" I raise my arm to punch him.

"Hey." He lets go the board, spreads his hands wide. I'm breathing hard. My nails dig into the palm of my clenched fist. "Take it easy, Sab!"

I lower my arm.

I feel stupid and he knows it.

"I was only going to carry it for you."

56

"I can carry it myself."

"OK, OK, don't be so touchy."

"Sorry," I mumble.

"Could I have a go some time?" he asks.

"Sure – I'll teach you. Come to my unit, er ... my house tomorrow if you like."

"OK." Troy grins. Somehow in my mind he replaces the images I've been having of Skin. His eyes look into mine for a minute.

"In return I'll take you out in my boat if you like."

I remember my dream.

I crack a grin. "Great."

We walk over to the others. Troy introduces me.

"Ringo and Lyxa you know," he says.

I nod and say "Hi".

I punch my sister lightly on the arm. She's wearing a white frock. "Does Pa know you're out?"

She scowls and looks embarrassed, tells me to shut up.

"This is Frog," Troy says. "We were at school together."

I hold out my hand. Frog is the guy I saw in the Net and Skimmer in the red cap. He's tall and thin with acne. His eyes are round and protruding. He shakes my hand limply, looking down his long nose at me.

"I heard what you did," he croaks.

"What?"

"Outside the Skimmer. I know some self-defence tactics myself."

"Yeah? What ... Taekwondo?"

Frog gulps as if he's swallowed something nasty. "Taekwon ... what?"

I grin. "Taekwondo ... it's an ancient Earther martial art."

"Er ... yes ... well, I expect we call it something different here. Anyway, we must have a contest sometime, although of course, being a girl we wouldn't be evenly matched. Even so, it might be interesting, don't you think?"

"I'll make allowances," I tell him.

He smiles froggily as if he thinks I'm being funny. "Why do you wear those strange clothes?" he asks.

"Why do you?" I look at his baggy Levis and grubby T-shirt.

"Oh..." He looks confused.

My sister takes his arm and pulls him towards her. "Don't be so beastly, Sabra," she says.

When the ship finally arrives it's like nothing I've dreamed of. I've been a few places, seen a few things but nothing ever like this.

It seems to be made of gold instead of the dull, silver-grey titanium of Earth-ships or the flat smoky black of interstellar space clippers. At one end a steepled tower is ablaze with a thousand lights; at the other, a transparent dome glitters blue and silver and aquamarine. You can almost feel the crowd holding its breath as she comes in, humming, hovering and rotating before she settles on the pad like an orchestra of light.

The noise dies down and the bulbs gradually dim to a soft golden glow. I've heard about these travelling carnivals that roam the galaxies but never thought I'd really see one.

I stand with my face pressed to the fence. I really fancy going aboard. I feel weird. As if something calls. As if something's in there waiting for me.

But I've no idea what it can be.

As we watch, the hatches whisper open and a figure appears. It stands in the doorway and makes a signal to the waiting trolleys. At the back of the ship double cargo doors open and unloading begins.

We watch the crates coming down. Some have force-fields, fluorescent in the semi-darkness. Animals roam within. Weird noises drift across the landing pad. Roars, little screams of fear and anger. We can see dark shadows pacing up and down. My heart reaches out to the creatures inside. I know how it feels to be shut in a cage when all you want to do is be free.

Two men struggle down the slope with a great tank slung between them. Inside, water catches the moons-light. It glitters like silver. Something lies motionless on the bottom.

Asleep maybe?

Or dead.

Steps come down from the auxiliary hatches and a

string of people disembark. One is tall, giant, like the indigenous race of Arrixa. Others are short, misshapen by human standards. One carries another on his shoulder. The freaks and flotsam of the galaxies I've heard them called. They walk across the pad to the administration building and disappear inside.

It's really dark now. The moons have gone behind a cloud. The fire is just a glowing ember, like a sparkworm waiting for its prey.

Troy's beside me. "We're going – want to come with us?"

Back at the Net and Skimmer we sit and listen to the juke. Down a few beers. Someone comes over and selects a King number. I think about that last night in the fun palace.

It seems a million years ago.

Lu sits close to Frog. "I understand Earth's very crowded these days," he says to me. "I'm going to college next year and I'm very interested in life on other planets."

He's a pompous creep. I don't know what Lu sees in him.

"Go to Earth and find out," I tell him.

"Oh, no," he croaks. "There's so much need for educated people here. I hope to go to Mainland and work for the Gummant party when I've got my degree."

I turn to Troy. "How come a friend of yours is such a prig?"

Troy grins. "Take no notice – he likes people to think he's clever. After all, he hasn't got much else to offer." He slaps Frog on the back. Frog coughs and almost chokes on his beer.

I laugh and sit closer to Troy. I want to put my arm round him but feel I might be rushing things.

I notice people are looking over at us. I thought they'd be used to me by now.

"Why do they still stare at me like I'm some freak?"

"People here are always suspicious of strangers," Troy says. "They probably think you're a Gummant spy."

Everyone laughs.

"And there's a lot of resentment about the new distillery," Troy goes on. "I guess they know your ma works there."

"Yeah – my pa mentioned that. Why *did* they bring in workers from Mainland?"

"Gummant party policy, I guess."

"Don't worry, Sabra," Lyxa pipes up. "That's why I'm not really allowed in here. My father's had a lot of hassle lately because of his involvement with the project." Lyxa looks around nervously at the guys sitting by the bar. A couple of them scowl at her, then look away. Lyxa's face goes red. "See what I mean?"

"Want me to sort them out?"

"No," she says quickly. "If there's any more trouble my mother will lock me in my room. I'm not supposed to come here. Thanks all the same, Sabra."

"How about us all going up on the Heights tomorrow?" Troy says. "Sab's promised to teach me how to ride that board of hers."

"I'm sure it's quite easy," Frog says.

"I'll come and watch," Lyxa says in her sweet voice.

"You'll never be as good as her." Lu sounds resentful.

"Come on, Lu – you'd be as good if you'd stuck at it."

Lu shrugs. "I've got better things to do."

Yeah, and I can guess what, I think to myself.

"Won't you come then?" Frog looks at her with his poppy eyes.

"If you want me to, Frog dear."

I feel like throwing up. I don't know what my ma would say if she knew Lu was in love with a reptile.

We meet the next day on Narran Heights. The sun beats down on our heads like fire. I've left my leathers at home and wear only shorts and a vest. I still feel vulnerable but I'm getting used to it. The view from the Heights takes my breath. Out to sea, the mass of scaffolding round the half-built distillery looks like some floating prison cage. From here the patrol boats are toys. Smoke from their funnels pollutes the sky.

From the wharf, a tanker sets off for Mainland with its cargo of Elix.

I strain my eyes looking for the tell-tale silver wake of a Siren but the sea is quiet, smooth and dark as a midnight sky.

From the path we can see the bright tents of the carnival pitched on the meadow behind the town. The houses of Narran look like they were built for dolls from where we're standing. Outside the council building a couple of strange Mitsubishi-cars are lined up in the street.

"I wonder what's going on?" I say to Lu.

"Some meeting of Gummant reps."

"How do you know that?"

"Pa heard some housewives talking about it in the market."

Here and there steam-tractors work the land.

Troy and the others wait by the stile. Lu runs on ahead and throws herself at Frog. They walk on, arms around each other. Lyxa trots beside them chattering. Her voice tinkles like a little bell.

Troy waits for me.

"Hi."

We stand and grin at each other. I take his arm in mine. His skin is tanned, muscles pretty hard for a boy. He's wearing black jeans and a vest with a picture of Snizzard on the front.

"Where's the best place?" I ask. "We need a smooth stretch."

I remember the smooth stretches on Summerland.

Troy frowns a minute.

"Past the old ruined farmhouse, I reckon. It's pretty dry and dusty up there but it should be OK."

"Is that near the excavations?"

Troy shakes his head. "No, higher up. We pass them on the way up though if you want to go look."

"OK."

We call out to the others we're making a detour. Frog's sweating so he and Lu lie on the grass to wait. Lyxa comes with us.

We skirt the meadow and walk the narrow footpath to the ruined town. It's in a dry river valley beneath the foothills of the volcano. Lyxa runs on down the slope. A song-lark flies, startled, from its ground-nest.

The walls of the old town have been reduced to rubble.

I walk among the lichen-covered stones.

"Looks as if a tidal wave or something hit it," I say to Troy.

He shrugs. "No one knows really. There's a theory that the town was invaded by Mainlanders and the inhabitants fled to the hills."

I climb up on the remnants of a tower, hand over hand, getting a grip with my feet wherever I can.

Troy stands at the bottom.

"Hey, Sab. Be careful, those stones are pretty loose." As he's speaking my foot dislodges one. He ducks out the way and stands there looking worried.

I look down at him and grin. One day I'll tell him about the blackened ruins of Earth cities where I spent half my childhood.

On the top I can see over the remains of the town. The walls of the old houses are eroded smooth by the sea winds of Narran. Here and there long-houses still have half their roofs. The timbers are split, rotted. They remind me of a wreck I saw once, aqua-diving in the Garian sea. At one end of the main cobbled street a whole pile of timbers and rubbish lies in a heap. It looks as if it's been swept there by a giant broom. The whole place smells of decay. Piles of earth where the archaeologists have dug down are like the termite-hills of the plains of old Earth. The place gives me the creeps. It's almost as if I can hear ghosts sighing through the ruins.

I climb back down.

"It's really weird," I say to Troy. "Creepy."

He stares at me until Lyxa comes up. She's holding a stone with little shells stuck all over it. "This place gives me the creeps, doesn't it you?"

I nod and try to shake off my feeling of unease.

"They didn't find any bones or anything," Troy says. "So there can't be any ghosts." He makes a moaning noise in his throat. He waves his arms around and grabs Lyxa. She gives a little scream and hits him with her fists. She throws the stone at him but misses.

"Don't be so horrible, Troy," she giggles.

Laughing, we make our way back to Frog and Lu.

"What was it like?" Lu says, straightening her skirt.

I shrug. It's not really like anything I've ever seen before. "Just a few old ruins," I tell her.

I shade my eyes and look beyond the fields to where the volcano rises above the town. Its slopes are steep and densely wooded. The forest below has a line where a great swathe of trees has been felled.

"Why do they cut so many trees down?" I remember pictures of trees that grew on Earth once.

Troy shrugs. "Lots of reasons. To fuel the steam-boilers at the distillery. To fire the trawlerboat engines. We burn it on our fires in winter ... loads of things."

"Doesn't anyone think one day there might not be any left?"

Troy shrugs again. "S'pose not."

Climbing the hill the dark, volcanic soil is dry and dusty. The air is fresh and sharp, the breeze like a flutter-fly on my face.

Something's tickling my shoulder and when I look a huge, lacy hawker-fly's sitting there washing its face. I touch it gently and it darts away.

The flowers, dancing beside the path, are garnet-red.

"Is it OK to pick one?"

"Sure, why not?"

"There used to be flowers on earth," I say sadly. A

66

buzzer flies from its centre. I bury my nose in its velvet petals. It smells like Summerland.

Troy takes it from my fingers and sticks it in the strap of my vest. His hand brushes my arm. He grins into my eyes.

As we walk along, spotted coney-rabbits dash in front of us. They disappear into holes in the bank. Once, Troy grabs my arm. I go to pull away but realize he's showing me something. In a dappled clump of bushes I see the bright eyes of a rodeer.

"Do any of these creatures come near the town?" I ask.

Troy shakes his head. "Grimmits and wolfdogs come to scavenge the bins sometimes if we get a cold winter... Not often though..." He breaks off, staring at a long low wooden building built in a clearing.

"What's up?" I ask.

Troy points. "What the hell's that? Hey, Frog..." he calls.

The others stop and wait.

"What the hell's that?" Troy says to Frog.

Frog shrugs his bony shoulders. "Looks like a store-shed of some kind."

"Let's go look if you're curious?" I say. I put my board down and climb the fence.

"Hey...!" Troy runs after me. "Wait, there might be someone around."

"So?"

As we get near, a guy comes out from round the front. He's holding a flint-rifle.

"Buzz off, you kids," he yells.

It's like a challenge.

My hand goes to my belt. It's the first time I've done that for days. Swearing, I dodge behind a clump of bushes.

I turn to look if the others are coming. To my horror they're hurrying away. I'd have expected it of Damosians but not from any sister of mine.

"Sab, for goodness sake!" Troy hisses.

I motion him to crouch beside me. "Keep down, Troy, he's got some kind of a weapon."

"I'm not blind," Troy whispers.

"You may as well come out," the man shouts.

"If I go out with my hands up you can creep round and jump him from behind," I suggest. "No old guy threatens me with a gun."

Troy sighs. "Sab, there's no point in starting any trouble. Let's get out of here."

I can't believe what I'm hearing. "I thought you wanted to see what's inside?"

"I was just curious. It's not worth getting hurt for."

My surprise turns to amazement. But I can see he's serious. I shrug.

"OK." I creep out. I put my hands up, spread them wide. "OK," I yell. "We're going. You can put your damn weapon away."

We walk backwards to the fence so he can see we mean it.

The others are waiting in the wood.

"Sab, for godsake." Lu's almost crying. "Why do you always have to get into trouble?"

"What trouble?"

"Well, that guard with the flint-rifle..." She breaks off. Frog puts his arm round her and gives me a look. I narrow my eyes at him and he drops his gaze like they're burning him.

"No harm done," I say. "It's probably made his day."

"Anyway," Frog goes. He's looking a bit pale. Scared. His eyes are protruding more than usual. "I've realized what it's probably for."

"What ... clever dick?" I say irritably. The guard's really got right up my nose.

"It's probably a store-shed for the new distillery. My father told me he was having to cut down extra timber to make store-crates. I suppose you know all about the new distillery Sabra, your mother being an engineer and everything. I'm absolutely dying to get a good look at it. It's so surrounded by scaffolding you can't see a thing, even through eye-spy glasses. And I heard they're going to erect some kind of screen round it next. I wonder if you could get permission to take me over there. No one is allowed near at the moment though goodness knows..."

Jeez, will he ever stop?

"Shut *up*, Frog!" Troy says.

"Well, anyway, I'm sure that's what this building's for," Frog says. His wide mouth droops sulkily.

We walk through the trees in silence. I think Lu's ashamed of being a coward.

It's gloomy inside the wood. Lu pretends to be scared and clutches hold of Frog's arm. Fat lot of good he'd be in a crisis.

Shafts of sun filter through the whispering leaves. They're all shades of emerald and jade. Swing-monkeys call and chatter across the branches. Sky-birds too. We see their bright flashes of colour. Their noise reminds me of market day in Narran. I almost fall over, looking. Troy clutches my arm as I trip. I regain my balance and shake him off. I'm still annoyed he didn't want to tackle that guard.

Then, suddenly, we're out in the light again. In front are slopes, stretching down to the valley.

"Down here," Troy points. In front, a long, narrow stretch of grass waits. "Will this be OK?"

"Great," I say. "Who wants to go first?"

"Show us first," Lyxa says before Frog can get a word in.

"Frog?"

Frog waves his hand. "No, show us the technique, I'm sure it's not that difficult."

Troy grins. "You go first then, huh?"

I show them how to start the motor, press the solar button then flick the ignition. The engine guns. I balance perfectly and skeet down the hill as if the hounds of Manja V are after me. I turn, shooting up a spray of turf and black, dusty soil. I buzz back to the waiting kids.

Frog's face is red with excitement. He hops up and down, croaking. "Great – let me do it, Sabra."

I tune the motor down a bit so it won't take him too fast first time. Frog steps on gingerly.

"Find your centre of gravity first..." He doesn't listen to me, flicks the gear. The board shoots off in a curve. Frog overbalances and is left sitting on the grass, eyes popping, face red. Everyone laughs. I run to catch the board. If it gets damaged, no engine for a hundred thousand million miles is sophisticated enough to replace this one.

"Sorry," Frog croaks sheepishly.

I show him again but it's no good. All he does is fall off.

"Let me try." Troy steps on the board carefully. I tune the engine down a bit more. Then he's off, down the slope, wobbling, arms waving like a wind-rotor. He goes a few hundred metres then falls off. He manages to grab the board. He walks back up the hill towards us grinning.

"Not bad eh – first time?"

"Try again." I tune the motor up a bit. He does it better this time. Falling off at the turn but managing to get all the way back in one piece.

"My turn, my turn." Lyxa jumps up and down with excitement.

"I thought you were only going to watch," Frog croaks spitefully.

"Well, I've changed my mind." She winks at me. "Woman's privilege."

Lyxa's great – a natural. After the first run she asks me to tune the motor up. Her dress blows out in the wind. After several tries she completes the turn and skims back.

I put my arm round her and give her a hug. "Well done."

She looks triumphantly at the boys. "It's really great. I love it." Her face is bright with exertion. Lu and Frog go off into the bushes.

Troy has a few more runs then we head for home. On the way back I tell them about Summerland. The fun we'd had when we were kids. To be away from the tower-blox for a couple of weeks was like the heaven of old-Earth legend.

We rest for a while. Sitting together, looking out over the sea. To the east the river mouth gapes wide, high sandbanks drying in the heat. The sun shimmers on the water like diamonds. I shut my eyes and try to conjure up the image of my Siren. The magic of her song has faded. It seems so long ago it's like a mirage. A dream-scape, a figment of my wishes.

A kind of heat-haze lies over us. It draws the sweat from our bodies. We lay in the grass listening to the

72

buzzerflies. The sky-birds wheel and dive above like space-fighters.

Idly I pick up a couple of stones. "These are weird."

Troy takes one, brushing my hand with his. "There's lots of these round here. Fossil-stones we call them."

I pick up another. It's got the outline of a tiny sea-steed imprinted on it.

Frog and Lu have reappeared. Lu straightens her blouse. Her lip-paint's smeared. Frog's got some on his face. He sees the stones in our hands.

"They're fossilized sea creatures," he says, knowing it all as usual. He squats beside me and takes one from my hand.

"No," I say, "you really surprise me, Frog." I wink at Troy.

Frog ignores me. "A lot of this island was covered by the sea once, did you know? We learned about it in geology, didn't we, Troy?"

"Did we?" Troy says. He picks a stalk of grass and sticks it between his front teeth.

"Yes, surely you remember? You must remember our teacher Raz, she had the biggest ... yes ... well ... the archaeologists say that the only places that weren't covered by water were the upper Heights and the volcano. That for a period in its history Narran was quite a tiny island. That's before it was inhabited, of course."

"Yeah?" I say.

"Big deal," Troy says sulkily. I can see he's jealous because, for once, I'm listening to what Frog's rattling on about.

"Most of Earth was covered by the sea once," I tell Frog. "There used to be places people could go to see fossils and things but all the buildings were destroyed in the wars."

"Typical," Frog says. "If you're interested in history and stuff, Sabra, you should go to Mainland. There's a wonderful museum there. All the stuff they found in the ruined town." He turns to Lu. "I'll take you there one day, Lu sweetie. I'm sure you'd be absolutely fascinated by the..."

"No thanks," Lu says.

"Troy said there's a theory the town was invaded."

Frog shrugs his skinny shoulders. "No one really knows. There's a period in Narran's history that we know nothing about. The theory is it's something to do with the climate. And the fact that once Elix was discovered, a whole new industry grew up around the sea. There have always been fishermen, of course, but evidence suggests most of the population lived on the Heights." Frog looks at the fossil-stone again. "They found lots of these there..." He shakes his head. "They thought people collected them as treasures."

By my side Troy's humming a rock number. He's looking up at the sky with a bored expression.

I put my hand on his arm. I know how sensitive boys can be.

"Come on," I say. "Let's get back. You promised me that ride in your boat, remember?" I turn to Frog. "Maybe I'll visit that museum with you, huh?"

Frog looks at Lu. "Would you mind, Lu?"

Lu shrugs. "Please yourself," she says.

"I've never been there," Lyxa pipes up. "Can I come too."

I smile at her. "Sure," I say. "Why not?"

I can think of a lot of better things than being alone with Frog for more than ten minutes at a time.

Troy's Island

The others have to get back so it's just me and Troy for the boat trip. He's been on about some little island he's been visiting since he was a kid.

I take my skeeter back to the house, grab a sandwich. There's a note from Pa saying he's taken the washing to the public laundry. Would I make sure I leave the place tidy as we're having some visitors. I wonder who it can be? He's left a pot of something on the stove. I take the lid off. It's dead creatures floating around in some kind of sauce. I almost heave.

I sit by the shore to wait for Troy. I dabble my feet in the sea. The air is hot and humid. The sky is hazy. The outline of the distillery seems to float like a vision in the middle of Selkie Sound. The threat of another storm hovers like a promise of doom. I remember Troy saying the monsoon season's almost here.

It's not long before I see a red-and-white sailed dinghy coming round the cliff. She skims the waves like a javelin.

Troy beaches the craft and jumps out. He wears only a pair of shorts. His body is lean, bronzed. I go and stand behind him. My mouth is level with his shoulder. I rest my hand on his back, just above the waist of his shorts. His flesh is warm, slightly damp.

"What do you think of her?" he asks proudly.

"She's great." I grin. "I like her name."

ROCKENROLLER is painted on the side in red letters.

"Built her myself."

"Pretty good."

"It's what I do."

"Huh?"

"It's what I do – build boats with my grandfather, Skipperjon."

"I didn't know you did anything."

"Did you think I was just a bum then?"

"I guess so."

"Charming." Troy holds out his hand. "Jump in."

"I can manage." I climb in easy-peasy. "What do I do?"

"Nothing – just lie back and enjoy it."

But I can't sit back. I get him to show me how to control the ropes, the tiller. Watching the muscles of his chest makes it hard to concentrate. Once or twice he notices me looking. He grins as if he can read my mind.

Eventually I take over. Then *he* lies back and enjoys it.

The wind blows my hair back – right off my face. The salt-tang of the air draws moisture from my eyes.

I always thought skeeting was the greatest but, boy, this is really something else.

The only other boats in sight are patrollers. That's where I head.

"Hey," Troy says. He tries to take the tiller from me. "We don't want to go too near."

"Troy, I've got to see this distillery. It's been bugging me for ages. There's something really weird about it. Ma won't tell me so I've got to find out for myself."

As we get near we see a huge screen has been erected round the project. From the Heights you could just make out the outline. From here you can't see a thing.

It must be as high as a K-13 Warhawk.

I whistle. "Why have they done that?"

Troy's looking nervous. "I don't know. Come on, Sab, those boats are heading this way."

The noise of the machinery almost blows your eardrums. Hammering, screeching, wheels on rails, the whine of steam-drills. A temporary dock's been erected and a cargo-cruiser stacked high with planks of wood heads towards it.

"Halt!" A patrolman's voice booms across the water. "No unauthorized personnel – turn round or we'll shoot."

"It sounds just like home," I say with a grin.

Troy moves across and takes the tiller from my hand. I let him without a struggle. When it comes to dodgy manoeuvres I guess he's better than me. He turns the tiller so we move in small circles. "I told you," he hisses.

I crouch in the bottom of the boat. "For godsake get down."

"I don't think they'll shoot. They're just bluffing." Troy's voice sounds brave but he looks scared as hell.

"Go in closer then."

"You're joking."

"I want to get a good look at that cargo boat."

He sighs. "OK, then." He turns the tiller so we sail in a wider circle. Then we go in closer.

"This is your last warning, turn round or we'll shoot."

Suddenly, I get an idea. I stand up.

"Sab!" Troy says. "Are you nuts?"

"I've come to see my mother," I yell. "Engineer Argosa." I can see some guy in uniform with some kind of primitive loudspeaker. He's standing on the bridge.

"He can't hear me, Troy, get in nearer."

Two other patrol boats are approaching fast.

"We're getting out of here," Troy says. "Now!"

"I've come to see..." I yell louder. Suddenly there's a flash and a rush of hot air past my ear. I duck down quick. "I thought you said they wouldn't shoot!"

"I was wrong." Troy turns the skiff. The wind catches the sail and we skim away. "You OK?"

"Sure – I've had nearer misses than that." I wish I had my leathers all the same. "What's all the fuss about, Troy?"

He shrugs. "Don't ask me. Maybe they think we've come to blow the damn thing up. To tell the truth," Troy goes on, "I don't really care. It's caused so much trouble. Everyone blames the Gummant."

"Well, I'm damned if a few men in Gummant uniform will scare me off – I'll get on it somehow, even if it kills me."

I look back. The steamers have gone back to their circular patrol.

"Still want to go to the island?" Troy asks.

"Sure."

When we are well away from the patrollers Troy sighs with relief. "You know, I never really thought they'd shoot."

"Why not?"

"Well, we don't have much need for guns here. There's hardly any crime. A few visitors get drunk in the summer, Honda-bikers mainly, on vacation. They cause a bit of trouble but that's all."

But it all seems pretty simple to me. They've got something to hide and I want to know what it is. I'm not like these island folk who want to be left alone to get on with their lives. Excitement, danger, it's life breath to me.

I look at Troy. His profile's grim against the wide blue sky.

It's not long before we reach Troy's island. Somehow the pleasure of the day has gone. I take the ropes from Troy. The wind is strong and I need my muscles. It's good to feel them being used to some purpose after all this time. I'm glad I've carried on working out.

The island's really tiny. White-gold sand fringes the ocean. On a rise in the ground a clump of red-fruit bushes grow beside a ruined temple. A coral reef separates the beach from the sea.

"Can I take her now?"

"Sure."

Inside the reef the water's as clear as the ice floes of Meridium Alpha. Bright sea-fish swim. Orange, Day-Glo green. A shimmer of silver and gold. I think of the Siren, of her silken tail. I let my hand trail over the gunwale.

"I shouldn't do that if I were you," Troy says urgently. "There's rhana-fish, they'll have your fingers off."

I take my hand out slowly. It's like a test.

I pass.

Troy lowers the sail and we drift to the shore.

"Does it belong to anyone?" I ask, jumping out. I haul the boat up on the sand. It feels warm and soft between my toes.

"Dunno, I've been coming here for years, no one's stopped me. There's great fishing from the beach on the other side."

I make a face. More dead creatures. Everywhere I go.

I leave Troy fussing with the boat and walk across the sand to the ruined temple. There are only two columns left standing. The green and yellow lichen makes stardust patterns on their surface. The others lie crumbling. Brown vine-weed strangles them. The place feels really creepy. Old religions always make me shiver.

Round the base are steps, the remnants of a wall fallen and crumbled with neglect. Through the broken slabs, grass and blue-faced flowers grow. Inside there might have been rooms, tiny windows with the remains of weather-beaten shutters. A bush grows incongruously from the wall. Ripe red-fruit, shaped like bells, hangs temptingly. The breeze seems to sing a lament as it choruses through the leaves. Songs of the dead reach out to me through aeons of time. It's really weird.

I shiver.

I sit down, elbows on knees, looking. I pick a fallen piece of stone. Some of it crumbles in my fingers.

Troy comes up behind me.

"I'm sure this place is haunted," I tell him.

He looks at me. "Yeah – it is a bit weird."

I remember a planet I was on once where ghosts dreamed on every street corner. No other Earthers could see them. Only me.

"Who came here do you think?"

Troy shrugs. "I think it was just a place where people worshipped."

I stand up and walk round the columns, touching their rough surface. In the middle of a small rock-strewn courtyard is a square stone. Some kind of altar. On it I can just make out a carving. I get my knife and scrape away some of the lichen. It's a picture of a sun, a planet and its moons. There's something else – a fish I think. Or maybe a Siren. The outline's too blurred to tell.

"Do you want to see the rest of the island?"

Troy's words break into my daydreams. "Sure." I don't like this place but I don't want to leave it either.

We walk round the shoreline. On the other side great black rocks stick out from the water. They're covered with pink and yellow climpets.

It's a place for Sirens.

For sea caves and song.

Troy shows me where he used to fish. He'd built a hut on the beach once but storms blew it down.

"I haven't been here for months," he says. "I'll come back one day and rebuild it."

I shiver. There's a cold wind this side of the island. Suddenly, I want to get away. "Let's go back to the temple."

We walk back to the cove. I lie down on the sand. Troy picks one of the red-fruit from the tree. We share it. Giggling. The juice runs down my chin, staining my vest the colour of blood. Troy gets a cloth from his pocket and tries to wipe it off.

We lie side by side, melting in the sun. I screw my eyes up against the glare. Sky-wheelers dive, their wings catching silver in the light. The sound of waves is like a lullaby. I turn languidly and rest my chin on my hand. Troy's eyes are closed. Long lashes sweep his cheek. Beads of sweat sparkle on his upper lip. Not for the first time I wonder what it would be like to kiss him.

As I lean forward he opens his eyes to look at me. So I lean down, closer, closer, until I can see myself reflected in his pupils.

Later we doze, the heat lulling our dreams.

I don't know how long we're there but when I wake the sky is dark. A great bunch of cloud has suffocated the sun. A hem of light edges the cloud with silver. As I watch the cloud darkens and spreads, covering the whole sky. Out beyond the reef white tips foam the waves. Beside me Troy is curled. I pull my arm from under his shoulder and shake him gently. He stirs and stretches. As he opens his eyes and sees me he smiles.

"You know what, Troy?" I say. "You're fantastic."

He blushes with pleasure.

"The weather's turned," I tell him. "I guess we'd better go."

He jumps up. "Hell! Come on, Sab."

As he speaks I feel the wind freshen from the north and drops of cool rain hit my face.

I help Troy push ROCKENROLLER into the water. As we glide away I look back at the temple. Is it my imagination or are shadows watching?

"We might just get back before the storm hits," Troy shouts. The sail comes alive and we gather speed. We head out to sea. As Troy turns the boat the wind catches us sideways and throws me off balance.

Troy springs forward and grabs the strap of my vest. The boom swings wildly, just missing his head. "Hang on. This is going to be rough."

I can see the great wave behind but I'm not quick enough to warn him. The skiff whirls round and round like a piece of garbage swilling down a drain.

I hear my name cried in anguish above the wind. I don't know if it's Troy or one of those island ghosts calling me back.

I feel the cold blue ocean hit me.

I'm falling, falling...

The dark shape of ROCKENROLLER's hull gets

further and further away and I know that as sure as gas-planets haunt the desolate outer regions of the solar system...

I'm drowning.

The Sirens

I don't know how far I go down before they come to me. I know my lungs are bursting. Noises like phantoms echo in my ears and forests of vegetation weave in front of my eyes. Shoals of sea-fish eye me hungrily as I try to swim. I lunge desperately for the surface. But my strength is gone.

I'm losing consciousness.

Helplessly drifting down...

The first thing I hear is their song. It comes to me through the ocean deeps to calm my mind and tame my wild heart's beat. I stop struggling and wait.

Then there are soft, insistent hands reaching out for me. I hold out my arms. I feel the reassurance of their touch on my fingers. They support me, guide me. I'm relaxed, on the edge of a dreaming sleep. Dark, undulating bodies brush me. Long hair and green-silver tails touch me like caresses. Their songs are taking me to the haven of their love.

They know who I am.

I've looked for them so many times and now they've come.

I'm being taken through a dark tunnel. So dark I can hardly see their shadows. Then the water is rushing past me as they bear me upwards. It's getting lighter. Brilliance shatters my vision. Brightness dances.

I break the surface.

I don't even gasp for breath.

I look around but they have gone.

I'm in a vast cave. It's big enough to house a thousand families. High enough to shield a Sky-master.

Warm ripples wash the sand where I lie. The walls sparkle with fluorescence. Greens and blues flash flares. There seems to be no way out.

Or in.

I take off my knife-belt. I wring out my shorts and vest. I spread them on a rock to dry. I sit at the ocean's edge and squeeze the moisture from my hair. I fling it back. Sand, like tiny black crystals sticks to the ends.

The air is warm, sensuous. Breezes drift. I stand up. I jog around a bit. Do a few press-ups.

I decide to explore. See if there's a way out. The

back of the cave seems to stretch to infinity. The floor is littered with rocks. Some have been used to make low walls, dividing the ground into sections. The air is sharp and clear.

I feel as if I could live here for ever.

About a hundred metres in I feel fresh air coming from above. When I look up I can see the sky but there's no way to get there.

Everywhere is evidence of humans. Cracked pots, fish-bones. In one corner is an old wooden chest. Half its lid's missing. Inside's a few tools, some torn and tattered bits of clothing. I take one out but it falls to pieces in my hands. There's broken furniture made from driftwood, shell plates generations old. I wonder if they've all been brought in by the sea. Under a rock I see something gleam and when I heave it aside it's a golden ring. It fits my little finger.

I walk back to the edge of the water. I perch on a rock.

I wait.

They come back gradually. A child is the bravest. She has a sweet face, soft like the petals of a flower. Her golden hair floats behind. I sit still as stone. My hands are spread so she'll know I'm no threat.

Her eyes are sea-green.

She smiles and touches my leg with her little webbed fingers. I lean down and stroke her hair. She climbs from the water to sit on my lap.

Then others come.

They gather round. I slide into the water so they can touch me. I never thought there would be so many. They run their hands over my body, through my hair. They talk to each other in high, excited voices. The sound reminds me of the wind over sand, far off songs in a mid-Summerland night's dream. I must have been stupid to leave my translator on Earth.

But we don't need words. The images they send to me are as clear as Earth moon's sky. They tell me I can live here for as long as I need. That I'll be safe. There'll be air to breathe and food to eat. That my children will live with no fear.

A couple of them disappear. They come back with shells full of alga. From their hands it tastes wonderful. Makes me feel great. Strong again.

More Sirens come. They bring things to show me. More human relics. Combs and mirrors made of polished motherpearl. Bottles, sea-bleached bits of driftwood. A stone with a carving of a planet, its sun and moon. A phantom of an idea is forming in my brain but is gone before I can catch it. Deep down I know what they tell me but I can't think straight. My mind is seduced with wonder.

After a while I get anxious about Troy. My ma will go spare thinking I've drowned. Just when she thinks she's rescued me from life on Earth. I want to stay here with my ocean sisters more than anything in the universe. They don't need any language known to tell them that.

I put on my clothes and use one of their combs to run through my hair. One brings me a piece of trawlerline and I tie it back.

I tell them it's time for me to go.

They shake their heads. Some begin to cry an ocean of tears. They pull their hair over their faces like shrouds of sorrow. I tell them I will always be on the shore. Waiting. To help them if they need me. To hear their songs.

They shake their heads and cry more.

At last, their leader, an elderly creature with greying hair and shrivelled, drooping breasts holds up her hands. They all fall silent. She turns to me. Her hands touch mine. In my mind I see mutinous waves and sea-lashed walls. There are people lined up on the shore, huddled together like refugees. I see floods and drownings and shining moons. Then there's peace and calm and sea-green flares that light the darkness. I frown and shake my head.

One day I'll work it all out even if it kills me.

I tell them my heart is breaking.

There are soft arms around me. I hug them back. I touch their hair, their sweet faces. I cry so much my eyes almost float from my head.

They take me gently. Into the water. Down through the thousand fathoms of darkness. Then up towards reality.

It's twilight. The storm has blown itself out and the sea is calm as death. The sky is streaked with purple. On the shore I can see my ma's cottage sitting on the dunes, waiting. The windows are lit as if to guide me home. Siren songs still echo in my ears. They've promised me safety, refuge, a life of ease. But a life of ease isn't for me. I know it. I tread water and turn to thank them. But they're gone. All I see is a ripple on the water, a flick of silver, a shadow-dream beneath the surface of the sea.

I strike out, swimming hard against the tide. By the time I reach the shore it's almost dark. The night is warm. Soon a million stars will be looking down at me. The twin moons of Damos spying on my grief.

I lie face down on the sand, my head in my arms.

I cry like I've never done before in all the days of my life.

When I wake the sun is coming up. A great ball of red that turns the sky to blood. My skin is stiff with salt, my face crusty with tears. I lie and think about my dream.

Then I get up, shake the sand from my hair, and make my way along the shore towards home.

They're all there. Ma. Lu. Pa. Troy and some old guy who's his grandfather. Two strangers are there too, sitting either side of my mother. When I go in they jump as if they've seen a ghost.

My ma's the first to reach me. Tears brim her eyes. "Sabra! Sabra!" She holds me close. "We thought you were dead." I stand, my arms by my sides, as if I really am.

Then Pa comes. Relief streams down his face.

"It's OK," I say quickly, hating to see him upset. "Everything's OK."

Even Lu comes to hug me.

When Troy holds me it's like he's the reason I needed to come back. When I look in his eyes I see he's had the same dream as me. But I know we can't tell anyone. I know they wouldn't believe me any more than they believed him. So I say I swam back and was so knackered I slept on the beach. And it's true.

I did.

In the corner the two strangers watch.

Troy introduces me to his grandfather.

"Sab." He puts a hand on my shoulder. "This is my grandfather, Skipperjon."

I say, "Hi, Skipperjon," and shake the old guy's hand. His grip is firm, hands rough with hard work. His eyes narrow at me shrewdly.

"Heard a lot about you, Sabra," he says.

"Yeah?" I look at Troy. He grins and wipes his eyes. "Who's the guys?" I ask my ma.

They're standing close behind us. They're two of her colleagues staying for the weekend. When my ma goes outside they follow her like they're scared she'll do a runner. I go and sit with her. They stand by a feather tree talking to each other but looking at us.

"Who *are* those guys, Ma? They give me the creeps."

"I told you, colleagues, they fancied a weekend off."

"They're acting like they're your bodyguards."

"Nonsense."

Just as she's hugging me they come over.

"Time to get back, Argosa," they say.

"Do you mind?" I tell them. "Me and my mother are having a private conversation." I put my hand to my side.

She touches my arm. "It's OK, Sabra. It's really OK."

But I don't believe her.

"You're not in any trouble are you, Ma?"

She laughs. "Of course not, darling."

"Ma...?"

She begins to look angry. "Just leave it Sab, will you?"

So I shut my mouth. I know she'll tell me when she's ready.

When they're gone I walk along the shore with Troy.

"Sab," he says. "That's got to be the worst experience of my life."

"Yeah?"

"Yes," he says. "I thought you'd drowned."

"Didn't you know they'd save me?"

"How could I? Loads of people have been lost at sea. Both my parents died when a ship capsized on its way to Mainland. Why weren't they saved?"

"Maybe they only save the ones who hear their song?"

Troy looks thoughtful. "No. Others hear but they don't understand. That's why they're scared."

We stop and look at each other.

"Yes," I say.

What Troy's said seems to fill in a bit of the puzzle I've been trying to fit together ever since I came to this beautiful, treacherous planet.

Back at home I go to have a bath. I'm rinsing myself off when Pa comes in.

"Sabra, you sure you're OK?"

"Sure, Pa – no problem." Then I say, "I'm really worried about Ma, what's up with her?"

Pa shrugs. "She's just working very hard I think."

"She's really uptight. Didn't you notice?"

"Sabra, she wasn't here for long. And as soon as we knew you were missing that's all we talked about."

"Who were those two guys?"

"She told you, didn't she?"

"Said they were some guys she works with."

"Well then, that's what they were."

"I didn't like them."

Pa laughs. "Sabra, you never like anyone."

"That's not true." I throw a shell-full of water at him. He dodges out. Then he puts his head back round the door.

"By the way, we might go away for a holiday."

"Who might?"

"Myself and Lu and your mother. You too if you want. It's her idea."

"Good, she could do with a break. Where you off to then?"

"Mainland probably. Fancy coming?"

"No, thanks."

He shrugs. "Please yourself."

"I intend to," I say.

Pa sighs and goes out.

Later I go back to the library. Ringo's there. She's sitting at the desk this time. I'm glad the creepy male's not around.

Ringo smiles. Pleased to see me I can tell.

"Are you OK, Sabra? We thought we'd never see you again."

"Can't get rid of me that easy."

She sees the ring on my little finger.

"Ooo," she says, "that's pretty. Did Troy give it to you?"

I grin. "Found it," I say.

She smiles back. Something, a spark of trust, passes between us.

"Lucky you," she says.

I tell her I've come for some books on their solar system.

She frowns. "I don't think we've got any here. I'll ask Mr Bumpa when he comes in though."

"OK," I say. "Thanks."

Outside, I meet Lyxa on her pedal byke.

"Come for a drink," she says. "Let's celebrate your return to the world of the living."

I hop on the back and we pedal off down the street.

There's a crowd outside the Net and Skimmer. One or two eye me and Lyxa with hostility. Lucky I'm wearing my leathers.

"What's up with that lot?" I say to Lyxa, glaring at them.

Lyxa shrugs. "Some meeting or other. Everyone's up in arms about the new distillery. My father says we might have to go away if it gets any worse."

"Where to?"

She shrugs. "Dunno. My mother's getting really nervous. Someone tried to break down our gates last night."

"Want me to come and stand guard?"

Lyxa smiles her sweet smile. "No, thanks, Sab. My father's going to try to get home for a while."

We go in and order our drinks.

Outside someone's shouting, telling the crowd they should tackle the Gummant.

"Why should we take low wages when that scum are getting rich at our expense?" I hear them yell. Through the window I can see a newsmag reporter clicking away with his camera. The crowd are shouting and waving.

Lu comes in with Frog. She's looking a bit pale.

"What's up, Lu?"

"Those people frightened me," she whines.

I feel ashamed she's my sister.

Frog squats down next to me.

"Sabra!" he croaks. "I've heard about your marathon swim. Did you know I was champion swimmer in my last year at school? You're very lucky not to have been attacked out there in the ocean, you know? The beach near your house is renowned for the abundance of swarks. And my cousin, staying here for the summer holidays one year, thought she saw a Siren on the rocks at Narran Point. You know they're said to hypnotize people with their songs, have you ever...?"

Lucky for me Troy comes in.

"Phew." He sits down close to me. "What a mob. Someone's called the sergeant to sort them out."

"They're really not doing any harm..." Frog goes on. "People must have the right to air their views, we are supposed to be a democracy, you know."

Troy laughs. "Since when?"

"Well, at the last elections it was quite clearly the

people's wish that the Gummant should be left to deal with matters of state.''

''That's rubbish,'' Troy interrupts. I'm looking from one to the other. For once I can't think of anything to say. ''Half the Narranese couldn't be bothered to vote. It's only since the new distillery's been on the cards that anyone's cared what's going on.''

''Come on, you two,'' Lyxa says. ''Who cares what the adults do. Just let them get on with it.''

Lu's looking up at Frog with adoring eyes.

Troy takes a swig of Elix and sits there looking moody.

''Are you all coming to the carnival tonight?'' Frog asks suddenly. ''It's the opening night. They're having a firework display. There's several new acts this year. I understand they've got a wild s...''

''Yes, Frog,'' we all chorus. ''We'll come.'' Then we all laugh loudly. Even Frog.

We get angry looks from the barman. I look daggers back. We're not doing any harm. Let him come and tell us off and see what he gets.

He soon forgets about us though. Some of the mob have come in and are ordering drinks. They still look angry and talk loudly amongst themselves. I see Lu press herself against Frog. She whispers something in his ear.

''We're going,'' they say, getting up. Lyxa goes with them.

Troy walks home with me. We keep our arms round each other. It feels good.

Along the shore my eyes search the ocean. The tide's running high and fast. There's a sharp edge to the wind.

"Summer's almost over," Troy says sadly.

"What goes on around here in winter?"

"Nothing much. The trawlerboats are mostly laid up for overhaul."

"What do their crews get up to?"

Troy shrugs. "Some work in the old distillery, others go out fishing. Some just bum around. The monseason's worse."

"Why?"

"Because it rains non-stop. Skipperjon and me can't do any work, neither can anyone else much. I hate it. Mind you..." He pulls me close. "This year you'll be around."

I hope he isn't getting any serious ideas.

My pa's out so I take Troy to my room. He laughs at my old Sunday bear until I get mad and stuff it under the bed. He takes my old-Earth books off the shelf. Reads some of the legends.

"Hey," he says, "they had Sirens on Earth too."

"It was just a myth," I assure him. "Men invented it. It represents the male fear of female domination."

Troy laughs. "Oh yeah...?"

"It's true."

He laughs again. "You Earthers do have funny ideas."

Annoyed, I take the book from his hand.

"Thanks," I say.

I put the book beside the bed and lie down with my head in his lap. We stay like that, listening to the sounds of the ocean.

"I hear they've got a captive Siren at the carnival," he says suddenly.

My heart does a quantum leap.

I sit up quickly. "No, you're kidding?"

"I heard someone say they captured it last time they were here."

I jump off the bed. I grab my jackets from the floor.

"I'm going to find out if it's true."

Troy stretches and yawns. "It doesn't open till six."

"Well, I'm going *now*."

I rummage in my trunk. Out comes my side-arm, wrapped in its oiled cloth. At the top of my cupboard is a box of ammo. I strap it to my belt.

"Sab ... what the hell?"

But I'm off. Down the staircase three at a time. I grab my skeeter and vault the gate.

I gun the motor and skim along the beach as if the dragons of Baraxus are at my heels.

I hear Troy shout. His voice is taken by the wind and scattered across the ocean to where the Sirens wait.

My hair flies out behind me. My heart drums a message along the shore.

Don't be afraid.

I'm coming.

I'm coming.

I'm coming...

The Carnival

By the time I get there they're just opening up. There's a crowd at the gate. They push, jostling for tickets. I don't have any bucks in my pockets so I sneak round the back of one of the tents. There's a fence. Climbing's easy. I keep low, it's no problem. I pat my hip just to make sure my side-arm's still there. It feels like an old friend.

To the left is the Big Top. That's where most folk are headed. The huge, wheeled cages are lined up behind.

I can smell the animals' fear. I hear their impatient pacings. Once or twice one touches its force-field and sparks fly. I creep between the cages and the tent. From one I see the bright tiger-eyes of a Sabre cat smouldering in the corner. I've seen trax of it hunting in the snow-mountains of Rimas. My heart feels sad. I'd like to let it out but know it couldn't survive in this climate.

Swing-monkeys scream and chatter. They set up a din as I go past. I look round. There's no one about. I wrench a chain from one of my jackets and chuck it high. It breaks the field. Sparks light up the night. The monkeys go quiet. Then they scamper out. Their hairy faces look my way, green eyes blinking. They disappear into the dark. Their tails wave like banners of freedom.

I grin.

Signposts point the way. One says Freak Show, another indicates side-shows and refreshments. A smaller one says Aquarium. My pulse thuds as I head that way.

The tent is long, yellow-striped, narrow. Bright lamps frame a wooden hoarding. They illuminate paintings. One's of a Siren sitting on a rock combing her hair. I stand and look at it for a minute. The brightness of the lights makes my eyes water.

There's a girl sitting in a transparent box by the entrance. She's dressed up in some kind of clown's outfit. Sparkly boob-tube, wide aquamarine trousers. She's filing one of her fingernails.

I lean close.

"Hi."

She smiles. "Hi – you from Earth?"

"How did you guess?"

She nods. "Your gear, you don't look like a native."

"Who does?" I say.

"What's that under your arm?" She points to my board.

"Skeeter board," I tell her. "Ever seen one before?"

She shakes her head. Then she takes a mirror from a bag strapped to her waist and examines one eyebrow.

"What's in there?" I ask casually, indicating the tent. "Anything worth seeing?"

She shrugs. "Not really. A few boring, smelly old fish. What's supposed to be a wild Siren but I don't think it's a real one. Some old thing with a fish tail on, I reckon."

"Why's that?"

"Well, they're supposed to sing, aren't they? This one's never opened its mouth. And it smells. It just sits there looking miserable. They're supposed to be dangerous, aren't they?"

"You tell me."

"Well, their song's supposed to hypnotize you, make you do things..."

"Yeah...? Maybe I'll take a look."

I try to peer inside the tent but it's gloomy. All I see are shadows of unhappiness.

"Anyway," Boob-tube goes, "most of it's a big con."

"Yeah?"

"The giant's from Arrixa so she's not really a giant, is she? If you see what I mean. No one there's under three metres, are they? And the hairy Earther's got some kind of accelerated hormone growth which isn't any big deal, is it? The Simosian twins are genuine but who wants to see two pathetic creatures with four heads between them, I ask you?"

"I guess people must do or else you wouldn't be here, would you?"

Boob-tube shrugs. "S'pose not. It's my first season with this outfit. Ran away from home."

"Home?"

"Mars base XII – hate the scorching place." She takes some kind of weed from under the counter and sets light to it. She takes a drag and puffs out blue smoke.

"Ever been to Earth?" I ask.

"You must be joking."

"Well…" I say lightly, "think I'll take that look inside, OK?"

"Got a ticket?"

I rummage around. Unzip all my pockets, careful not to show my side-arm. I feel in the back of my leggings. "Lost it," I say.

"Oh, yeah?" Boob-tube looks at me sideways.

"It's true." I grin and spread my hands.

She drags more smoke from the weed. It streams out through her nostrils, turning green as it hits the night air. Then she shrugs. "Why should I care?"

She presses a button and I go through the turnstile.

Inside are rows of illuminated tanks. There are bright fish. Sinuous snakes. Rhanas with fierce, black teeth and a dwarf water-dragon from Aliddan that looks as if it's seen better days. One's got something inside that looks like a swark. I feel like shooting its brains out. Other tentacled, beaked creatures swim about looking miserable. They're not what I'm searching for. I feel sorry for them but I can't take the whole universe on my shoulders.

My heart's thumping so loud I'm sure she can hear.

At the end of the row is a screen. On it there's writing. Earth script. It tells the Siren legend. There are other paintings. Shipwrecks. One of a huge tri-masted sailing ship with some guy strapped to the mast as he sails past an island. A dozen Sirens sit on rocks, their hands stretched out, their voices raised in silent song. I remember reading the story in my old-earth books.

Suddenly the tannoy booms.

NOW COME INSIDE AND SEE FOR YOURSELF.
DON'T BE AFRAID. IT CANNOT HURT YOU.
OUR SECURITY SYSTEM IS SECOND TO NONE.

I look around but there's no security system I can make out.

It's dark inside. At first I see nothing. When my eyes get used to the gloom I just make out a tank. There's someone sitting on a rock. Murky water laps its base.

Behind the glass her shape looks distorted. As I stare, lights come on and recorded ocean sounds fill the air. Her head is on her breast, bent in dejection. Her hair covers her face. Her tail, curled round the rock, is dull. Lifeless. Sad.

The sound that comes from my throat is like pain.

She raises her head slowly to look at me. I get as close to the glass as I can. I press my hands against its cold surface. My eyes swim. When they clear she's looking at me.

She knows I've come for her.

She knows her sisters wait.

Round the back of the tank is a ladder. I put my board down by one of its legs and climb up. I stretch my hand towards her. She reaches out and touches it. Her flesh is dry, cold. The skin between her fingers, scaly. As she raises her head I see a scar across her throat.

"I'll be back," I whisper although I know she would hear me even if I didn't open my mouth.

She smiles. Sadly, hopelessly. No sound comes from her lips.

I go out past a few kids oohing and aahing at the creatures in the tanks. A man's voice booms from outside.

COME AND SEE OUR WILD SEA-SIREN.
QUITE SAFE. THE ONLY ONE IN CAPTIVITY.

I want to punch his stupid face in.

As I leave, the crowds are flocking, jabbering excitedly. All the wonder of seeing the carnival ship arrive, the excitement at the exotic figures coming out, has gone. The carnival stinks. Its glamour and brilliance are as much a lie as the danger of the seductive Siren song that lives within my dreams.

Someone grabs my arm. "Sab! I've been looking for you everywhere."

It's Troy but I can't speak to him. My throat's closed up with sorrow. I pull away.

"Sab! Wait."

I hear him running after me but I have to get out. I can't let him see me cry.

But he catches me up. Grabs me. He stares at my face, then puts his arms round me whilst I sob.

"They've taken her voice away, Troy, the stinking creeps!"

I really hate him to see me cry but there's nothing I can do. Seeing that Siren has killed me.

People are pushing past. Troy pulls me behind the Big Top. He holds me close again. He strokes my hair.

"You shouldn't have gone to see it, Sab."

"Why not?" I pull away and wipe my face on my sleeve.

Troy shrugs, not knowing any answers. Then he

says, "There's nothing you can do, Sab. Why upset yourself?"

"Who's upset?" I sniff and wipe my face again. I feel studs scratch my cheek. Troy takes a grubby cloth from his pocket and hands it to me.

"You," he says.

"Me? I'm fine. And anyway, there's a damn lot I can do."

Troy looks wary. "What?"

"Get her back to the sea of course. You should see her, Troy . . . she's dying."

"But Sab. . ." Troy starts to protest.

"But nothing. What's the matter with you people? Lyxa gets attacked by some maniac and her ma doesn't want any publicity. People from Mainland are taking your jobs and all I hear are a few people objecting. You have to fight, Troy, and I'm going to fight for that Siren if it's the last thing I do on this stupid planet."

I hear him sigh. "What can you do?"

I walk away. If he doesn't know then I'm not going to tell him.

He runs after me again. "Sab. . .?"

I whirl round. "I'll think of something, Troy, and if you're too much of a coward to help me I'll find someone who will."

I see anger flame in his eyes. "You know I'm not a coward, Sabra. I just think it's stupid to risk your neck, that's all.'

"They risked their necks for you, didn't they?"

He shrugs.

I snort in disgust. "Well, who needs punks like you anyway?"

He stands and watches me go.

Then I hear his footsteps running, feel his hand on my shoulder. "OK," he says. "I'm sorry. Of course I'll help you."

"Don't..."

"Sab," he interrupts. "I said I'm sorry."

We stand, eyes blazing, while the moons of Damos hang watching. He puts out his hand to touch mine. "OK?" he asks.

I relax. "OK, punk."

Troy grins.

"I need the others too," I tell him.

"Are you kidding? Frog'll be scared to death and the girls won't be any good."

"Don't be stupid, of course they will. And persuade Frog, OK?"

He salutes. "Anything you say, sir."

"I'll meet you back here at midnight."

"Where're you going?"

"I've got a call to make."

I turn and walk quickly away. Troy's watching me but I don't turn round.

The first thing I do is find the Freak Show. There's so many people it's hard to find your way around. I get pushed along with the crowd until I finally get to the tent. I'm shoved through the turnstile. No one asks for a ticket.

Inside, the exhibits sit in little cubicles. Hairy men I've seen before. The Simosian twins sit reading four newsmags, oblivious to the gawking hordes. Narranese children squeal and point. They suck candypops. In one cubicle is a sand-monkey with two sets of back legs. Next to him's the fattest Ralvoan fangspider I've ever seen. I'd like to put it down the trousers of whoever mutilated the Siren.

The atmosphere's oppressive. The place stinks. The sooner I find what I'm looking for, the better.

In the last cubicle is the Arrixan giant. She sits in an armchair reading a Karactan tabloid. She's dressed in some kind of silken frock the colours of a hawker-fly's wing. A serpent's tattooed on her hairless scalp.

I'd wondered why a giant was in a freak show. Now I see why. She's got the most serenely beautiful face any giant ever had. Most Arrixans are ugly as hell.

I lean over the barrier.

"Hi." I make the Arrixan greeting sign. I knew one day I'd be glad I studied their culture in school.

She looks up sharply. A grin spreads across her wide face. Her golden eyes twinkle in the dim light from the candle-lamp.

"Hi, kid. Where d'you crawl out from?" Her voice is deep and booming. The sides of the tent vibrate.

I grin. "The woodwork."

"What's your name?"

"Sabra," I tell her.

"How come you speak my language?"

"Doesn't everybody?"

"You kidding? Where're you from?"

"Earth."

"Never been there," she booms.

"Don't blame you," I say.

She looks at me, waiting for me to go on. I smile. "I need a favour."

She looks suspicious. Female Arrixan giants are always suspicious. "What?" she goes.

I tell her.

She thinks a minute. Then she smiles. "OK, to tell the truth I'm so bored I'd wrestle a garbage-dragon for a bit of a laugh. And you know I've always felt sorry for that poor creature. She's not like the other aquatics, they haven't even got brains."

I look around. "What are you doing in a place like this?"

"Ever seen a giant who looks like me?"

I shake my head.

"Besides," she holds up a deformed foot. Only seven toes instead of nine. "I was born like this. And I'm dark skinned, even for one of my race." She raises her eyebrows and shrugs. "And I'm female. Everything on Arrixa was against me. These so-and-so's

pay well and I get to see the universe. Why shouldn't ▶
be here?"

"No reason," I say hastily, not wanting to antag-
onize her. I know how touchy giants can be.

"What are you doing here?" she asks.

"Tagged along with my ma. Nothing much to do
on Earth."

"So I've heard," she says. "Except try to survive."

"Right." I grin. "Where shall I meet you then?" By
this time people are watching us curiously.

"By the Sabre cat's cage ... midnight. OK?"

"Great."

I make the sign and slip away.

Things have quietened down a bit outside. The first
circus performance's just begun. A brass band honks
from the Big Top. Some twit in spangled tights is
leading a string of golden unicorns into the ring.
They're prancing and dancing, their horns gleaming
in the glare from the spots. I remember seeing wild
ones on the plains of Geron 4. I bet they wish they
were back there.

Patting my side-arm for reassurance I walk through
the gate.

Outside the carnival field I gun my motor. It's a
good run through town and up the hill. The streets are
deserted. One or two Elixaholics stagger around but
apart from that there's no one.

Outside Lyxa's I press the buzzer. Lyxa's voice comes over the intercom.

I tell her who's here.

"Your Pa home?" I ask.

Lyxa tells me he isn't.

"Going to the carnival?"

"I don't know," Lyxa says. "Mum's not well..." She sounds fed up.

"What's up with her?"

"Just the worry of everything, the doctor says. He's given her some tranquils."

"Worry of what...?"

Lyxa says she doesn't know.

"Can I come in a minute?" I ask.

"Sure." I hear a click as she unlocks the gate.

"Will you meet me outside the house?"

"What for?"

"I need a favour."

There's silence for a minute. "OK ... I owe you one, remember?"

Truth is – I'd forgotten.

She's waiting by the side door when I arrive.

I tell her what I want. Not why I want it though. Not yet.

"Sab..." she goes. "I don't know..."

"I'm going to take it anyway, Lyx."

"What if my father finds out?"

"Not scared of him, are you?"

"A bit..."

"He won't find out, I promise you." I put my hand on her arm.

"OK, I'll get the keys."

"Can you get a couple of blankets ... a bottle of water?"

Lyxa looks puzzled. "I'll try."

While she's gone I creep along the side of the house. Standing on my board I can see in one of the windows. Homer's study. The rolled-up plans are still on the table. There are models of sea vessels on the sideboard and there's a drawing board over by the window. On it's a plan of a weird-looking ship. It's like something I've seen a picture of in an old-Earth book but I can't think what.

Lyxa behind me makes me jump. My hand flies to my side.

"Take it easy, Sabra," she whispers. "Why're you so jumpy?"

"Who's jumpy?" I say.

She hands me a key.

"Thanks." I give her a hug. "You go back in now."

"Not likely. I'm coming with you."

"You might not like what I'm going to do."

She shrugs. "Whatever it is it'll be more exciting than sitting reading newsmags."

She's not kidding.

I've never driven a groundmotor before but I guess once you know the principle the rest is easy. Lyxa gives me a few hints from watching her pa. She insists

116

on helping me push it from the garage and halfway along the drive in case Mrs H. hears the engine start.

She points to the gas gauge. "There's not much fuel. This month's delivery hasn't arrived from Mainland for some reason."

"We'll take the chance," I tell her, putting my skeeter under the front seat.

We cruise through town and out towards the carnival field. I look at my tikker. It's ten-thirty. The carnival shuts at eleven.

I park the limmo behind the Big Top.

"Want to find the others?"

"If you like."

"I'll stay here with the motor, OK? Can't risk someone pinching it. Tell them to meet me at the Sabre cat's cage. Five minutes to midnight."

"OK . . . Sabra. . .?"

"Yep." I look around in case anyone's getting suspicious.

"Tell me what you're up to," Lyxa says, looking wary.

"You'll find out soon enough."

I help her over the fence then get back into the limmo. I lean my head against the back of the seat. I take deep breaths. It's a long time since I've done anything like this.

I send my thoughts to the Siren so she knows I'm coming.

Just as I'm getting relaxed I hear voices. I dodge down.

"Whose motor's this then?"

"Dunno. No one's got permission to park here."

Two guys come up from behind. Flashlights shine. I sit up and wind down the window. I keep my other hand on the gun.

The lights dazzle my eyes but I don't flinch.

"Hey..." I go, "do you mind?"

"What're you doing parked here?"

"Waiting for the governor. What's it look like?"

"Is this his limmo?"

I laugh. "Is this his limmo? You kidding? Who else on Narran's got one like this?"

"Where is he then?"

I can just make out a swarthy face, a cap tilted to one side.

"Gone to visit some ... er, lady. He just told me to wait till he gets back."

"Why didn't he park round the front?"

"You crazy? Have his *wife* find out where he is?"

The two guys grin. I see them nudge each other.

"Got any ID?" one asks.

"Only this..." I pull my side-arm. So quick they hardly see my hand move. It feels great in my fingers.

The swarthy one gasps. They both step back.

I put it back into my belt. "OK, OK, don't sweat. I just carry it to prove who I am."

"The governor's driver?"

"Who else? He's not too popular nowadays, what with the trouble about the new distillery and all. Needs protecting. I hope you won't ... er ... tell anyone about this."

They switch their flashes off. "Don't worry, we won't say a word."

"Thanks." I smile sweetly. "I hope he won't be all night, it's damn cold."

"Want someone to keep you warm?"

I almost throw up. Male vanity never ceases to amaze me. Anyway, these guys could be the ones that slit the Siren's throat for all I know.

I keep my voice steady. "What, both at once?"

They nudge each other again. "If you like," Swarthy says.

Through the windscreen I can see the carnival lights starting to go out. The tikker on the dash says twenty to twelve.

"Some other time maybe." I finger my gun.

They mumble something about teasers and shamble off into the night.

I put the limmo keys into one of my breast pockets and zip it tight. I grab Lyxa's blankets and the flask. I climb the fence. I head for the Sabre cat's cage. It's in there chewing the leg off something. It growls from its throat. I stand in the cage's shadow. Waiting.

"Sab?" It's Troy, whispering from the darkness.

"Troy. Over here."

They all speak at once.

"Hey," I hiss. "Keep your voices down."

"What's all this about, Sabra?" Frog croaks. "I'll have you know if I don't get at least eight hours sl..."

"Godsake, Frog, shut your mouth!"

"Don't be such a bully, Sab." Lu puts her arm through his.

"OK," I say, ignoring her. "This is the deal."

Even though it's dark I can see Frog's face go pale. The others, even Troy, look decidedly nervous.

"Rescue a *Siren*," Frog splutters. "You must be mad. I'm not going to risk my life for some half-human creature that might..." He starts to hop away.

He feels my side-arm in his back. "Stay here, Frog. I need you."

Frog freezes. Then turns slowly and sees my gun. His eyes almost pop right out. "What's that?" he croaks.

"What's it look like?"

"Sabra," Lu hisses. "You were supposed to leave that on Earth."

"Sorry," I say, not meaning it. I look straight at Frog. He lowers his gaze. A drop of spit oozes from the side of his mouth.

"She won't use it, Frog darling. She's never killed anyone yet." Lu pushes the gun to one side.

"There's always a first time," I tell her.

Frog puts his hands into the pockets of his Levis. "Wh ... why ... do you n-need me?"

"You said you knew some tactics. Thought they might come in useful."

"Well ... I'm not really very..."

"Shut up, Frog," Troy says impatiently. "Let's get on with it, Sab. If Frog doesn't want to come I can fight, you know?"

"I know that Troy." I look into his eyes for a moment. I see fear in them. "Frog...?" I ask.

Frog shrugs his puny shoulders. "All right."

My gun slips sweetly back into my belt. I smile at Ringo and Lyxa. "OK ... not scared, huh?"

"A bit," Ringo admits. "Why do you want to do it, Sab?"

I touch her shoulder. "Because she never hurt anyone in her life. And she's dying, Ringo. We can't let that happen, can we?"

"Hundreds have died," Frog says. "One more won't..."

I finger my side-arm and he shuts up.

"Sab, I've heard they can..." Ringo says.

"Whatever people say, Ringo, there's nothing to be scared of. I promise you. I don't know how she got into this carnival but she belongs in the ocean and I'm going to see she gets back there. OK?"

Ringo nods and smiles. "OK... Sabra?"

"Huh?"

"Are you sure she won't sing?"

"I'm sure. She won't sing. Not ever." I turn away so they can't see the pain in my eyes.

Frog begins to say something but the Sabre cat's getting jumpy so he shuts up. It's finished its supper but still sounds hungry. It pads towards the front of the cage. Its eyes gleam.

At five past midnight the giant comes.

She's just a dark shape at first. She limps along. Her shoulders tower against the sky. She looks warily behind.

"You there, kid?" Even whispering her voice is loud.

I step from the shadows. I make the sign. "Here."

I introduce the others. Frog looks as if his jaw's going to drop off. Lyxa and Ringo hold hands and stare up at the giant with scared eyes. Troy grins uncertainly as he stands on tiptoe to shake her hand.

I tell her the plan.

We walk in single file to the aquarium. Troy carries the blankets. Lyxa the flask of water.

The place is in darkness. The tent flap's sealed for the night. I slit the ties with my knife and we go in.

"Haven't you got a torch?" Frog complains, tripping over. "How are we expected to see anything?"

"You crazy?" I hiss. "Feel your way." He grabs the back of one of my jackets and hangs on tight. Maybe it was a mistake to bring him after all.

When we get to the Siren's tank the others hang back.

"Look," I say impatiently, "she won't hurt you."

"Supposing she starts to sing...?" Lyxa's voice is shaky.

"She can't, they've taken her voice."

I hear everyone gasp.

They stand and stare at the figure lying motionless at the bottom of the tank.

"I think it's dead already," Frog whispers, going nearer.

My heart drums a beat of panic. "No...!"

I go towards the ladder but the giant pushes me aside. "I'll get her out. You wait here and take her from me."

"Spread the blankets, Lyxa," I say.

Lu's hanging on to Frog's arm, pretty useless as usual.

"Lu," I hiss. "Go outside and keep guard."

"Me?"

"Yeah, you!"

I hear my sister sigh and go off mumbling something. Frog hops after her.

I tap on the glass, press my face against it. She must know I'm here. She must have heard me telling her I was coming.

She stirs. She flicks her tail but there's no flash of silver. Or of gold. I tap again and she raises her head. Her hair weaves as the water around her stirs. I see recognition in her eyes. I point upwards to the waiting giant reaching long, long arms down into the water...

Without hesitating she moves upwards. The water

flows off her body like a bride's nightgown. Their hands meet. Small webbed fingers grasp huge, broad giant hands. She's lifted up, up. Up.

I take her from the giant and lay her gently down.

On the ground we wrap her in the blankets. Lyxa and Ringo are pale with fear but they don't hesitate.

The giant lifts her again. "Which way?"

I lead them back to the entrance. The giant's bent almost double as she carries the Siren gently towards the flap. Suddenly we hear voices.

"We're actually looking for my baby brother," Frog's saying loudly. "Well ... he's not actually a baby, he's almost ten years old. But he said he was coming to the carnival and when he didn't come home my parents asked me to look for him. They're going absolutely spare. Mind you, I told them he's always going off on his own, nothing to worry about. We found him once down by the wharf watching the trawlerboats unload and he was only..."

An impatient voice interrupts. We see a torch flashing. "How did you get in here?" a voice says. It's the security guy I met before.

"In?" Frog says. "We've never been out. We've been here all evening. My father sent a message via the sergeant. There're so many interesting things to see here, don't you think? It's much better than last year, I mean they..."

"We'll just take a look inside. Hey!" the security guy goes. "This flap's been cut!"

I hear a scuffle, then a grunt. Motioning the others to stay where they are, I dash out. I hear Troy behind me.

One of the guys is lying on the ground. He's rolling in agony. The other's got hold of Lu. Frog's sitting on the ground rubbing his foot.

"Get your hands off my sister!" I leap forward. The security guy's arm swings. His torch catches my cheek. I feel the skin shred. I fall and roll over, up again, side-arm like a friend in my hand. The guy's face drops a mile.

"You again! I said you were up to no good." He lets Lu go. She runs to Frog. Troy's standing over the guy with the injured pride.

"Frog!" Lu throws her arms round him. "That kick was wonderful. Have you hurt your foot? Oh, do let me look."

"A bit." Frog winces as Lu kneels to rub his ankle.

I get a coil of electro-wire from one of my pockets. I wipe the blood from my cheek with the back of my hand.

"Lu, put this round them." She leaves Frog and winds the wire round the man's wrists and ankles. He struggles.

"I'll kill you," I threaten, jabbing the gun into his ear. He freezes. Lu connects the wires and sets the fuse. "If you try to get it off it'll ignite and blow you to hell," I warn. Lu does the same to the other guy.

Troy's hauled Frog to his feet.

"Thanks, Frog." I pat him on the back. He almost trips. "You must show me that move sometime."

"Be glad to, Sabra." He puts a hand on Troy's shoulder and hops on one leg. "I actually learned it from..."

But I don't hear where he learned it. I go back into the tent and beckon the others.

"It's OK. Come on..."

"How long can it stay out of water?" Lyxa asks when we're on our way.

"I don't know." I touch the Siren's face. Her eyes are closed. Her skin is dry. "She can breathe air but I don't know for how long." I smooth back her hair. My hand's covered with blood. It stains her forehead. "We'll get you to the ocean as quick as we can," I promise her softly. Her eyelids quiver and I know she hears me.

Troy runs on ahead and opens the limmo-door. The giant bends double and bundles her into the back.

I tell Ringo and Lyxa to sit with the Siren. "Troy and Frog in the front with me."

I turn to the giant, putting my hands up to hers. I tell her how to deactivate the wires. Then I say thanks in a voice she knows comes from the bottom of my heart.

She pats my head maternally. "Any time, Earth-kid."

She shambles away over the fence. She disappears

into the darkness. I hear the Sabre cat hiss as she goes past, then the night is quiet.

We cruise through town with our precious cargo. The kids are silent. Troy sits close to me. His hand's on my leg. I hold one of his famous grubby cloths to my cheek. Once, he looks at me. I grin.

When we get to the coast road, Lyxa speaks.

"She's hardly breathing, Sabra."

"We won't be long now." I glance in the mirror. The Siren's head's on Ringo's shoulder. Lyxa holds one webbed hand in her own.

"She smells funny," Frog pipes up.

"So do you," Ringo says.

"Really. I don't think that's very nice, especially after..."

"You'd smell if you'd been shut up in a tank of filthy water for years." That was Lu. I don't know if she's heard Siren songs in her dreams but she might from now on.

"Lu...?" Frog starts to protest.

"Shut up, you lot," Troy hisses. He turns to me. "What happens when they find those security men, Sab?"

"Hopefully we'll be long gone and she'll be back in the ocean..."

"Yes, but they'll be able to identify us."

"Who? Us?" I grin and touch his leg. "Lyxa's been at home with her mother who's drugged up to the eyeballs with some stuff the doc gave her. We'll all swear we were somewhere else. It'll be their word against ours. Isn't that right, you guys?''

Ringo and Lyxa giggle and say yes.

"And who'd want to steal a Siren anyway?'' I go on.

Troy shrugs. "True.''

"Anyway,'' I say. "I'm used to interrogation. If they pick me up they won't get anything out of me. Besides, the giant's fixing things.''

"How?'' Frog asks.

"She'll think of something.''

We reach the top of the cliffs above Narran Point. I turn off the engine. Something tells me we've got to be quick.

The Siren's still motionless. Lyxa undoes the lid of the flask and holds it to her lips. Her mouth opens feebly. Lyxa pours water on her hand then gently rubs some into the Siren's forehead. She smooths back the hair that has fallen over the Siren's face.

Lyxa looks at me. Her eyes are full of sympathy. "We'd better hurry, Sabra,'' she whispers.

Troy and I lift her gently from the back seat. Between us we carry her down the long flight of steps to the shore. The tide's in. The water laps only a metre away. It's higher than I've seen it before. Lyxa and Frog, Lu and Ringo stand on the steps and watch.

We lay her gently down on the sand.

"What shall we do now?'' Troy asks.

"I'll handle it. You take the limmo back for me, OK?"

"But Sab...?" he starts to protest.

I reach out and touch his face. "Troy, I have to do this on my own. They won't come if everyone is here ... Please?" I lean forward and kiss him. He puts his arms round me and holds me against him. Then he lets me go. He pushes the hair away from my face. There's fear in his eyes. "You sure you'll be OK?"

"Come off it, Troy," I say.

"Your cheek's still bleeding like hell." He pulls the sleeve of his sweatshirt down over his hand and wipes the blood.

"It'll be fine," I assure him.

He lets go reluctantly and joins the others.

I wait until the limmo's gone. The wide sweep of its headlamps illuminates the top of the cliff. Then darkness. Along the shore I hear a skimmer call.

Then everything's quiet apart from the gentle lap of the surf calling her home.

I sit down and unwrap her gently. Her breathing is shallow. I place my mouth against her forehead. It feels hot. I put my arm under her shoulders. I pull her up so her head rests in my lap.

I wait.

Clouds scud across the moons. A few twilight-dippers wander along the water's edge. They ignore us. The cool air sends fingers through my hair. The sound of the waves almost lulls me to sleep.

It's not long before they come. Two at first. Heads bobbing. Their hands weave. The sea bubbles cast moons-light pearls into the water around them. Then two more. Then another.

I wave my arm although they know exactly where I am.

They come nearer.

Slowly. Cautiously.

I shift the Siren gently aside. I take off my clothes. Then I lift her up. I pull her gently towards the sea. Her tail flicks, makes a groove in the sand.

Soon I'm waist deep and the water takes the burden of her weight. She stirs, moving her head this way and that. Her hair weaves a spell of desperation around her thin shoulders. I float on my back, kicking out. The salt stings the cut on my face.

Then I feel them round me. They take her into the haven of their arms. There are gentle hands, murmuring voices. I tread water, then swim in circles.

The sky clears and I see them swimming away. They disappear one by one until the only movements are the wave tips and the only sound is the joyous singing of my heart.

At home, Lu's in the cooking room making a hot drink. My skeeter's propped up against the ice box.

"Thanks for bringing it back," I say, going in. "Was there any trouble?"

Lu shakes her head. She speaks in a whisper so's not to wake our pa. "Nope. Want a cup of brew?"

"Why not?" I sit at the table and put my feet up.

Lu brings a cup across. "Let me look at your cheek." She lifts the flap of skin. When I wince she clicks her tongue. "That's nasty." She goes to get some stuff from the cupboard. She bathes it gently. She's good at that kind of thing. She even had a doll once. "Lucky Pa brought some medi-plast from Earth." She tears off a strip and sticks it on.

The cut will be healed by morning.

We sit looking at each other across the table.

"What made you do it, Sabra?"

But what can I tell her? She wouldn't understand. I shrug. "Anything for a bit of excitement."

She sighs and finishes her drink. She takes her cup and rinses it. Going, she turns. "You're crazy. I'm glad we did it though. That Siren was...?"

"What?"

"Beautiful ... almost human."

"Being almost human makes you beautiful, does it?" I could think of a thousand species that wouldn't agree.

Lu goes red with annoyance. "Oh, Sab ... you still have that attitude problem, you know?"

"What attitude problem's that, Lu?" I grin.

She grins back. "Frog was wonderful, wasn't he? So brave."

"Yeah," I say. "Wonderful."

Next morning I go back to see the giant. I know it's risky but who cares? There's no one about. Maybe they're all out looking for swing-monkeys?

She's in her trailer mending her socks.

"Hey, kid," she says. I can tell she's pleased to see me. "Did you get her back to the sea OK?"

"Yep. I've come to say thanks again. Did you deal with those security jerks?"

She grins. "Sure did. Somehow I don't think they'll tell anyone. They'll say they were right over the other side of the camp when it happened."

I didn't ask her how she persuaded them.

"Been much trouble?"

She shakes her head. "Not much. The creature was past it really. They've got an amphibious Puff-devil waiting for them on Balengro 9. It was going to replace her anyway."

"What would they have done with her?"

"Fed her to the Sabre cat I suppose."

I shudder. The giant reaches into the folds of her frock and hands me something.

"Your wires – you might need them again one day."

"Thanks."

"Heard something about some swingers going missing too. Know anything about it?"

"Not a thing," I say, grinning.

Her smile's as wide as the sky.

I climb on a stool to hug her. "Good luck."

"You too, kid. Might see you again some time."
"Who knows?" I say.

On the way home I stop off at the library. I leave my board in the porch.

"Thanks for your help last night, Ringo."

"I quite enjoyed it. Will she be all right?"

"Hope so," I say.

"By the way," Ringo says. She crouches down and gets something from under the counter. "I told Mr Bumpa you were interested in our solar system. He found this in the stock room."

"Great!" I take it from her. "I'll remember to give him a kiss next time I'm in."

Ringo smiles. "You'll have to join first." She leans over the counter and touches my cheek. "You'll have a scar there, Sabra."

"It'll fade."

"Hope so."

I sit on the shore and spend an hour or so reading the book. It answers a few of my questions. I'm going to have to find something, or someone, who can answer the rest.

When I get home there's a Mitsubishi-car at the gate.

The Vacation

When I go in, my mother and the two guys she works with are sitting talking in the cooking room. There's some kind of argument going on. They stop talking when I appear. Upstairs, I can hear Pa banging around. A pot of something boils on the stove. I go to my ma and give her a hug. I nod at the engineers.

"Where's that scar come from?" Ma enquires. She touches my cheek. She looks tired, ill, in need of that vacation Pa was rattling on about.

"I fell off my skeeter."

"It's about time you gave that up." My father comes in carrying a travel bag.

"Why?" I ask.

"There's been some trouble at the carnival," he

says, ignoring my question. "Know anything about it?" He puts the bag by the door and goes out again.

"Who me?" I wink at Ma. She raises her eyebrows but says nothing.

"Yes, you, Sabra," Pa calls from the bottom of the stairs. Through the door I see him take another bag from Lu. He hauls it into the kitchen and puts it beside the other one.

"Don't know a thing, Pa." I grin at Lu. She doesn't smile back. Her eyes are red, face paint smeared. "What's going on?" I ask.

My mother starts to say something but one of the guys interrupts. "You're going on vacation," he says.

"Yeah?" I look at him. "Who says?" He's got beady black eyes like a weasel-ferret. I feel a hand on my arm and when I look round my ma's shaking her head at me and frowning.

"Sab, I thought we'd all go away on holiday. Didn't your father mention it?" she says.

"Yes." I nod. "But I'm not going."

In the chair Lu sniffs.

"Sabra, do come," Pa pipes up. "I thought you wanted to see Mainland."

I shrug. I do want to see Mainland but I'll go when *I* decide. Not when someone tells me to.

"I'm sorry," I say. "I'd just rather stay here if you don't mind."

Pa looks at my mother. His eyebrows are raised. She starts to say something else then changes her mind. She knows it's no good trying to make me do something I don't want.

So I make my excuses and go to my room.

Upstairs I look out my window. The day's oppressive. A haze of heat hangs over the horizon and fine drops of mist clothe everything in grey. It reminds me of earth. The sea is the colour of mud. There's a kind of stillness in the air like a threat of doom. Through the mist the fog siren calls across the water like a searching ghost.

I sit on the bed and thumb through the library book. In my gut the seed of realization settles and begins to take root.

I hear footsteps running up the stairs. Lu stands by the door. She's been crying again. Her hair's all messed up and one earring's missing.

"What's up, Lu?"

She stamps her foot. "It's not fair!"

"What?"

"Why is it you're allowed to do what you like but I've got to go on some crummy holiday!"

I shrug. "They couldn't make me go."

"Then why can't I stay here with you?"

I grin. "You'd love that."

She sits beside me. "Sabra, ask them please. I can't bear to leave Frog, honestly…"

"Come off it Lu, I'm sure there's someone more hunky on Mainland just waiting for you."

"I don't want anyone else." She begins to cry again.

I put my arm round her shoulders. "It'll only be for a couple of weeks, Lu. Look ... the weather's lousy here, something's brewing I can feel it. You'd be scared of a storm ... and Pa wants you to go, you know how Ma hates him to be upset."

Lu wipes her nose on the back of her hand. "But why should I have to go and not you?"

"Because you're only a kid."

She wrenches away and stands up. She stamps her foot again. "I'm fourteen and a half."

"So, you're fourteen and a half. Pa needs you, Lu. He doesn't need me. He'd be lost with no one to look after. Besides, Ma looks really tired. She needs a holiday more than any of us."

Lu sighs and looks resigned. "Will you tell Frog to wait for me?"

"Sure I will, Lu. I'll send him your undying love."

She scowls. "I hate you, Sab. You're such a smart-arse."

I get up and give her a hug. "That's the nicest thing you've ever said to me, Lu."

I hear her clumping angrily down the stairs.

I follow her down.

"Well," the guy called Jak says to me. "Are you coming?"

"No," I say. "I've already told you."

"We do think it better if you go with your parents," the other one says.

"Who cares what you think?" I take a step towards him. My mother dodges in front and stands between us.

"You won't like it here when the monseason starts," he says.

"I'll be the one to decide that." I blaze my eyes into his. All I want to do is punch his stupid face in.

"Sabra!" my father yells.

The whole thing's turning into a circus.

I feel my mother's hand on my arm. "Sab. Come into the other room. I'll talk to you alone."

The other engineer steps forward. "I'll come with you." I feel the tension like thunder in the air.

"Sit down, Hobart," my ma says. "We'll only be in the other room."

For some reason Hobart follows us and stands by the door.

Ma shuts it firmly in his face. "I don't like the way those jerks talk to you," I say to her.

"Ignore them," she says. She sits down on the sofa. "Sab, I really want you to come with us."

"Me? Oh Ma, you know it's not my scene. Anyway, why is it such a big deal? Anyone would think you're going away for ever."

"Sab, the Company are paying for us all ... I really wish you would."

I turn to her, flicking back my hair. "Ma, what is all

this? Why are those guys still sticking to you like glue?''

She laughs but it's false, I can tell. ''They think I need protecting, I suppose.''

I grin. ''They must be kidding.''

''Anyway,'' Ma says, ''they had to come here to see Homer so I hitched a lift. And they're taking the bags for us to the dock. Sab ... if I said that it was the most important thing in the world to me that you came with us, would you change your mind?''

I look at her long and hard. I really want to please her but I've been away too long. I have to be free. She knows that.

I shake my head. ''No,'' I tell her.

''Is it that boy?''

''What boy?'' As if I don't know.

''Troy.''

''Ma ... you know me better than that.''

''What is it then? Why won't you come?''

''Ma, I like it here. For the first time in my life I *really* feel as if I belong. I just don't want to leave right now. Not even for a couple of weeks. Maybe later on, when the distillery's finished we could backpack somewhere, just you and me, huh?''

My mother looks resigned. She knows better than to argue any more. She puts her arms round me and hugs me really tight. As if it could be the last time we see each other. I hold on to her. My heart drums a mysterious beat of fear. Those guys. The vacation ...

Ma's worried face. None of it's right. "Ma?" I begin. "Something's up. I wish you'd tell me."

She shakes her head. "Nothing's up." She puts her fingers to my lips. "I'll see you soon," she whispers.

Then I remember. I've got something important I've got to tell her. "Ma," I go. "I've been reading this book about the solar system ... I wanted to tell you something..."

She smiles and shakes her head. Outside I hear the Mitsubishi-car's doors being slammed. Hobart comes in. "We're ready, Argosa. Is she coming or not?"

"Not," I tell him.

Ma hugs me again and goes without a word.

When she's gone I feel like crying although I can't think why.

I stand at the window watching the groundmotor winding its way towards the road. I hear its engine droning away into the distance. The silence closes round me.

Not even Siren songs come to calm my pounding heart.

If being free means being alone I'm not sure I like it.

I put a few things in my bag and go off to find Troy.

Later we're sitting at the water's edge. We've been skeeting along the sand. The wind's got up and cleared away the mist. The horizon's dark with threatening clouds and the setting sun edges them

140

with blood. I've got my arm round Troy's shoulders. I've been telling him about the book.

"So, Damos once only had one moon," he says. "I've got a feeling we learned something about it at school."

"It's pretty obvious," I say. "Pictures of old carvings they found when they excavated the old town only have one."

"Yeah." Troy lies back on the sand. He stretches his arms over his head. "So now you've got this momentous bit of knowledge what you going to do with it?" He grins.

I sit and hug my knees. Then I turn my head to look at him. "I don't know. There's something else. Some gap in history. It all ties in somehow with the Sirens."

I feel his hand on my waist. "You're nutty about the Sirens," he says.

"Yeah," I say. "I suppose I am. You know I always knew there was something weird about this planet. Something hidden..."

Troy laughs. "Like what?"

"I dunno. I felt it right from the day we landed."

Troy laughs again. "You're the weird one, Sab."

I must be getting soft because all I do is punch him lightly in the stomach. He grabs me and pulls me down on top of him.

For a while I forget about everything else.

When I've walked home with Troy I skeet back along

the sands. The tide's out. In the Sound I can see the flickering lights of patrol boats. I'd heard in the Net and Skimmer the distillery's almost finished. Someone was talking about some strike up at the old place. Another about holding a demo.

Near home I jump off and kill the motor. I stand a minute but there's no sign of my ocean friends. It feels like a lifetime since I saw them. I watch night-birds fly. I take deep breaths of sea air. I know in my heart I belong to this place. I knew it from the moment I stepped off the shuttle and heard a song echoing across the flats towards me.

As soon as I go indoors I know there's someone there. The hairs at the back of my neck stand on end. I flick off the light and creep along the passage. I keep flat against the wall. I put my hand to my side but my gun's back upstairs in its hiding place. Instead I pull my knife.

The cooking-room door's open just a bit. I see someone's back. They're sitting at the table, head in hand. I kick the door open and jump in, crouched, ready for trouble. My knife flashes.

"What you...?"

Then I see it's my ma.

I put my knife back in my belt. "Ma?" I put my hand on her shoulder. She looks up slowly. I've never seen my ma crying before and the sight kills me.

I kneel and put my arms around her. "Ma...?"

She sniffs and wipes her face with the back of her

hand. She unzips one of her pockets and takes out a cloth to wipe her nose. She tries to smile.

"Ma, you should be more careful. If I'd had my side-arm I..."

"I know, Sab, I'm sorry."

"Ma, what you *doing* here? Where're the others?"

She makes me sit down.

Then she tells me.

And what she tells me makes my heart pound with terror.

Then, as she goes on, the sad, sad song of the Sirens begins to echo through the corners of my imagination.

And then it comes to me. The key to the puzzle I've been trying to work out for so long. Suddenly I know why Siren songs called to me across the flats. I know what they were trying to tell me when they took me to their sea cave. Why I knew that if I stayed there I'd be safe. And I know now for certain just why their voices have echoed, unheard, around these shores for countless generations.

And I know, as sure as there are dinosaurs in the forests of Cassiopi, that their music will haunt my dreams for ever.

"Hostages...?" I say a bit later. "Ma, are you kidding?"

My ma shakes her head. "No, Sab."

I shake my head. "No wonder they wanted you to persuade me to go with you."

"Yes. I managed to convince them your pa and Lu were enough. There was no need for them to have you as well."

I shake my head again. "And now they've taken them out there to make sure you still keep your mouth shut."

Ma bows her head. "That's right, Sab."

"Oh, Ma! How could you let them do it?"

"I didn't have any choice."

It's my turn to shake my head now. Disbelief and anger washes over me like a flood. "Jeez, Ma, why didn't you tell me?"

"I couldn't. All along they threatened that if I let on, you and Lu and your father would be killed."

I get up and walk around the room. I'm so angry the studs on my boots make sparks on the flagstones.

"But why did you stay? Why didn't you leave as soon as you found out what was going on?"

"I tried... That's when they began threatening me. Sab, I know it's my fault. I should have found out about the project before we left Earth. I've already told you that. But when they threatened me I thought I'd find a way out..." My ma shakes her head. "But I couldn't, Sab, do you think I didn't try?" She bangs her fist on the table. "You know, Sab," she goes on, "when it comes to a choice between your principles and the lives of people you love..."

"I know, Ma," I go and put my arms round her. My voice breaks into a thousand fragments. "I understand..."

There's silence a minute while we hold each other. When I pull away my face is wet with her tears.

"You know," I say eventually, "I knew there was something weird about that distillery. The screens, those patrol boats. And I saw a plan on Homer's wall." I sit back and put my head in my hands. "I should have asked more questions."

"I'm sorry, Sabra. I've let you all down badly."

"No, you haven't, Ma, we know you came here for a better life."

She snorts. "Huh, some better life."

"Ma," I say. "What I don't understand is why they don't send for some star-ships or something ... some of those clippers hold half a million..."

Ma smiles grimly. "No one would come. You know Damos is a tiny, unimportant planet. It isn't even a member of the Galactic Community. And who cares about some little world the other end of the eighteenth galaxy anyway? It's a job to get people to care about their own world let alone one most of them have never even heard of."

"And what do they think will happen to the rest of the people ... those on Mainland?"

My ma's eyes fill with moisture. "Sab, you know most of Mainland's only a metre or so above sea-level. I'm afraid there won't be anywhere for them to go."

"So the premier, the Gummant reps – so called *important* creeps will be OK – and to hell with everyone else?"

My ma bows her head and doesn't answer.

"Ma – how can they do that?"

She looks at me and there's all the sadness of the universe in her eyes. "You only have to read the history of a thousand human inhabited planets to know how they can do it," she says.

"How long do they think it will be before the waters recede?"

Ma shrugs. "No one knows. Months maybe ... years even ... there's no way of predicting."

Her face looks so tragic I know I must tell her.

"You know, Ma," I begin, "there's no need for any of this garbage, everything can be OK, I know it. I..."

Ma shakes her head again. "No, Sab, there's no way out. The scientists have predicted the asteroid will be here before the monseason begins. There's nothing we can do. I came back to warn you, to make you see you *must* come with us. The ship is being launched in two days' time."

"But Ma, I told you. There's no need..."

She frowns. "Sab, I don't understand?"

So I tell her.

We spend the rest of the night talking. I make a pot of

brew and we sit, clasping the mugs as if the warmth will give us life. Pa left in such a rush there's hardly anything in the cupboards but we find some bread and make a fruit sandwich.

When the moons disappear and light starts to creep over the roof, Ma says she's got to go back.

"I got Pa to tell them I was in my cabin, sick," she explains. "Then I slipped out and hid in a lifeboat on one of the supply vessels when they were changing watches. I pinched one of the fishermen's pedal bykes at the quay to get me here."

I can't help cracking a grin. Ma was right when she told me she was just like me.

But she doesn't smile back. "I've got to be back before dawn," she says. She looks at her tikker. "There's a supply boat leaving at six, I've got to be on it."

"Ma," I say. "You do believe me, don't you? You do understand what I've been telling you."

She smoothes back my hair. "Yes, Sab," she says. "You've always been able to see things other people can't." Her eyes fill. "But whether anyone else will believe you I really don't know. I wish I could stay to help you but I'm afraid they'll kill..."

"It's OK," I tell her. "I'll manage it somehow."

"I really wish you'd come with me."

"I can't desert my friends, now can I?"

"No ... one traitor in the family's enough..."

"Don't say that, Ma. You know you had no choice..."

I think of all the heroines of old-Earth history who'd had choices to make.

"Didn't I?" she says sadly.

"No," I tell her and hope she believes me. "Ma," I go on, "can't you get Pa and Lu back here?"

She shakes her head. "They're locked in their cabins until we sail."

"Look, if you let me come with you I'll get them out."

Ma shakes her head. A ghost of a smile flickers across her face. "No, Sabra. They might be being held hostage but at least they're safe."

She had one last request.

"Sab, promise me you'll wait until the ship has sailed before you warn people. If there's any hint that people know ... then they'll kill your pa and Lu, I know they will."

"Yes," I promise. "I'll wait."

"And if you change your mind..." She unzips a pocket and hands me her pass. I look at it then hold it out for her to take back.

"I won't change my mind."

"Keep it anyway."

I shrug. "OK."

"Sab, I don't want to leave you..."

When I kiss her goodbye I feel my heart break.

When she's gone I skeet along to Narran Point. At

the bottom of the steps I sit and work out what I'm going to do. Out by the rocks I see a dark head bobbing. Then another. In the early light I see a flick of silver. Songs ride on the wind towards me.

I pick up my board and climb the steps. At the top I turn. One has climbed on a rock and is combing her hair. The others swim around her. Then, as the fleet of trawlerboats comes from the harbour and heads out to sea, they disappear. And although their songs still echo through my heart I know, now, they'll be back.

I turn and head for town.

The Truth Behind the Legend

In Narran square there's a crowd gathered. A few folk stand in café doorways, mugs of Elix in their hands. The guy on the steps is waving a newsmag and shouting. There's even a few women deserted their cooking rooms to come and listen. There's a reporter writing stuff in a notebook and some guy with a camera, clicking away as if he's got the scoop of the century.

Troy's grandfather Skipperjon's standing by a stall selling vegetables.

"What's going on?" I ask.

He takes his weed-pipe out of his mouth. "This." He shows me a newsmag.

DISTILLERY TO BE COMMISSIONED TOMORROW is the headline. Underneath it says:

150

Gummant sources today revealed that the long-awaited new Elix Distillery off Narran Island is to be commissioned on Chrysday. No word has yet been given on the old Plant just outside Narran town in spite of lobbying by workers...

The story goes on to say how a week-long strike by distillers hasn't forced management into a statement and even a boycott by dockers loading supplies for the new distillery has had no effect. *The Gummant has merely brought in workers from Mainland to load the cargo* the newsmag says. In the opinion column the editor's encouraging the Narranese to carry on with their protest. *For years*, it says, *the workers of Narran have been exploited by the Gummant and by the Elix Company – now is the time to do something about it.*

I flick through the newsmag. On the back page, right at the bottom as if it's of no importance, there's a story about an amateur astronomer on Mainland. He's discovered a new star in the sky.

Getting brighter every day, he's said in a statement. *The most exciting discovery for years.*

He's not kidding.

I hand the newsmag back to Skipperjon.

"You should stay out of the way, Sabra," he warns. "A lot of these people know your mother works on the distillery."

I grin. "Thanks for the advice," I say.

Down at the boatyard Troy's painting someone's dinghy. When he sees me coming his grin's as broad as the horizon.

"Did you see the carnival ship take off?" he asks.

"No – when?"

"This morning. I went out to the flats with Frog."

"I couldn't. My ma paid a visit."

Troy puts the lid on the paint can and bangs it down with a stick. "Your ma? What for?"

"Troy, will you come back to my place? I've got something I want to tell you."

He looks at me shrewdly. Then he touches my hair, pushes it back behind my ear. "You OK, Sab?"

"Who me? Course I'm OK. Troy, will you come?"

"I'm supposed to finish this job."

"Troy, it's important."

He shrugs. "Skipperjon'll kill me, but what the hell…"

He puts the paint and brushes into the shed and locks the door.

On the way I tell him I saw his grandfather in the square.

Troy makes a face. "Not like him to get mixed up in that kind of thing."

"He was only listening."

Troy shakes his head. "Frog told me his father's organizing some kind of demonstration. Nothing like it's ever happened here before although it's about ime someone did something. I really don't know what's going to happen."

No, I think. But you soon will.

Along the shore the waves are angry. The wind whips the sand off the dunes. It hits our legs like stinger-flies. I put my arm round Troy's waist as we walk. I hook my fingers in the waistband of his jeans. I know our days of heaven are numbered. The sky looks moody, heavy with the threat of storm. I think about Pa and Lu locked up on the ship. I think about my ma.

"Is that true about the distillery?" Troy asks.

"What about it?"

"That it's being commissioned tomorrow?"

"Kind of."

"What do you mean ... kind of?"

"I'll tell you when we get home."

Troy gives me a funny look but doesn't say any more.

"I saw the Sirens this morning," I tell him.

"Yeah?"

"On the rocks past Narran Point. Three or four."

"Wow," he says. "Maybe they're coming back."

"They are," I say.

Troy looks at me again. He frowns and shakes his head.

At home I take him upstairs. When he starts to fool around I hold his arms.

"Troy, I want to talk to you."

"OK, what about?"

I get my sketcher from the cupboard. Troy sits with his chin against my shoulder. He's frowning.

"What's this, art classes?"

"Wait..."

I sketch their solar system. Chrysos the sun. Damos – Luna and Ananke, its moons. I press the button on my sketcher that makes them gold and silver.

"You remember the legend?" I say.

Troy shrugs. "Sure."

"How Chrysos saw Luna and had the hots for her?"

Troy nods.

"And when he captured her she got greedy and sent a flood to cover his kingdom?"

"Uh-huh."

"You don't know where the legend comes from?"

Troy shrugs again. "Haven't got a clue."

"Well, you remember I told you about Damos only originally having one moon."

"Yep." Troy's starting to sound bored.

"And now it's got two. Ananke, the original one, and Luna the second one. When she arrived, a great flood covered the land, yeah?"

Troy sits up. "How do you know that?"

"I figured it out. Ever heard of the 'wife' theory?"

He shakes his head. "Earthers don't have wives, do they?"

I smile. "No, but the theory was worked out when they still did."

"OK, explain it then."

"You know about asteroids ... lumps of rock and iron that orbit planets?"

"Uh-huh."

"Well, the theory is that sometimes their orbit brings them too close to a planet and its gravitational force captures it."

"So?"

"So, it becomes a planet's moon, tied to it for ever. Just like wives were supposed to be tied to their husbands for ever. So ... the 'wife' theory, see?"

"Right," says Troy beginning to look bored. He fiddles with one of my zips.

"You know the moons control the tides?"

"Sab, I'm not a complete dummy."

"OK ... well listen then. There's an asteroid heading for Damos. It'll be here before the mon-season. When it's near enough, it'll be trapped by the planet's gravitational pull and go into orbit with Luna and Ananke."

"How do you know that?"

I tell him what the scientists have discovered. "They've been tracking it for months. Conditions are just right for it to be trapped..."

Troy leans back. "Well, I guess that's pretty exciting..."

"Troy, you don't understand!"

"What?"

"Do you know what effect a moon has on a planet's oceans, on its land masses?"

"Well...?"

"Troy, when it gets here its pull will be so great the ocean will rise and cover almost the whole of the land surfaces of this planet just as they did when Luna was captured into orbit round Damos all those years ago."

I can see he doesn't believe me.

"I don't see how you can know all that stuff," he says.

"Troy, it's been happening for billions of years on planets throughout the universe. It's happened here before – that's how the legend of Chrysos and Luna came into being."

"How can you be sure? How can anyone...?"

"I am sure, Troy. Look ... it all figures. The deserted town on the heights. I knew it reminded me of something. I went diving once in the Garian sea. There was a town there that had been above the water before a marsquake caused it to sink. It reminds me of that, Troy. And, when you think about it, there are so many other things."

"Like what?"

"Like Narran's wildlife living so high up. How else could some species have survived a flood? Like that weird gap in Narran's history when no one seems to know what happened." I put my hand on his arm.

156

"Troy, that's not a distillery out in Selkie Sound. It's a huge sea-ship. It's been built as a refuge for the premier and Gummant reps and other so called important people so that when the floods come they'll survive."

Troy's eyes grow wide. "How...?"

"My ma was conned into building the engine. When she found out what it was for she tried to leave. Troy, they wouldn't let her. They've got Lu and my pa hostage and will kill them if she lets on."

Troy frowns. "Sab, you're kidding me?"

"I'm not, Troy, believe me I wish I was. That's why my mother risked everything to get back here last night. To warn me..."

Troy gets up and goes to look out of the window. He turns. He leans on the sill. "OK," he says, fear lurking in his eyes. "Tell me the rest."

And so I tell Troy what my ma's told me. About the Gummant reps arriving secretly at the distillery. About the supplies stored in the sheds up on Narran Heights. I tell him they chose Narran because of its position in the ocean and because it's off the shipping routes other than for traders in Elix.

"When's it sailing?" Troy asks.

"Tomorrow."

He shakes his head. "I knew those creeps were up to something." He bangs his fist on the windowsill. "So I suppose the rest of us drown, do we? Or do we take our pathetic belongings and head for the Heights..."

I shake my head. "The scientists say the asteroid's massive. My ma says maybe some of the wildlife will survive but there really won't be anywhere for people to go except..."

"Where?" Troy's face is a mask of pain and misery. He buries his head in his hands.

I go to put my arms round him. I lay my cheek against his hair.

"Don't you *know*, Troy? Don't you know what happened to the people all those years ago when Luna appeared? Don't you know where they went?"

He shakes his head.

So I tell him that as well.

At first he doesn't believe me. Then, I remind him about the goddess Sirena – how she represents all the Sirens. The statue at the harbour, the temple on his island with what I now know *was* definitely a picture of a Siren carved on the altar. I see belief dawning in his eyes.

"You mean that's why they worshipped them," he says incredulously, "because they saved..."

I nod. "Before the pioneers landed and persuaded them it was stupid to worship something that threatened your livelihood. You've only got to see a few Earth history trax to know certain groups of Earthers have always been intolerant of what they called pagan religions – especially if they interfered with something they wanted to exploit."

Troy shakes his head. "But how can you be so sure?"

"Remember what happened to me when I fell out of ROCKENROLLER? How the Sirens promised me safety? Remember what happened to *you*? All you have to do is listen to their songs, Troy."

Troy shakes his head again but I can see by his eyes he believes me.

"Sab," he says at last. He puts his arms on my shoulders and leans his forehead against mine. "You're really something else."

"We've got to warn everyone," I tell him after a minute or two's silence. "But I promised Ma I'd wait until the ship's sailed. If there's any trouble, they'll kill her and Pa and Lu."

"I've got a terrible feeling no one will believe us," Troy says dismally.

"They've got to."

"I know." He stands up suddenly. "I'll ask my grandfather. He'll know what to do."

"Troy, you can't, not until..."

"I know, but as soon as it's gone. He's bound to go and watch. I'll make sure I'm with him."

Later, when we've tossed a few plans around I walk to Narran Point with Troy. He's going to stick to Skipperjon like glue until the ship's gone.

At the bottom of the steps he puts his arms around

——— (159

me and buries his face in my hair. We stay like that for a minute. As we stand there I feel the sound of distant Siren songs invade my heart.

I kiss him then watch him go up.

At the top he turns and waves. Suddenly, I remember my last night on Earth. How they'd all watched me dodge up the four thousand and ninth parallel on my way back to the home-unit. How Skin had looked, standing there, twisting the jewel in his ear, the tears running down his face. It seems a lifetime ago. Now when I turn, there are no droids watching. No neons and sky-cars screaming overhead and no drip, drip of condensation from a hundred thousand billion breaths. There's no cacophony of noise from a thousand blaring commercials or the high pitched scream of blazer-guns. There are no bodies in the gutter to step around. All that's nothing but a bad dream. What I really see is the endless midnight sky of Damos. The moons – clear bright Ananke and Luna with her slowly disintegrating aura of tears. And what I hear is the low thunder of the silver-tipped waves and the soft lilt of the nightwader. And, if I'm lucky, the enchanted sound of a Siren song drifting across the waves towards me like the fanfare of our salvation.

Back home I sit in the cooking room drinking tree-apple juice. The remains of the sandwich I had with my ma lies curling on the table. There are no skivvydroids here to come and clean up. Outside, the wind dances against the shutters and sings through the eaves. I can hear the sound of the breakers. If the tide comes up any higher the place'll be washed away.

Above the noise I hear the sound of a groundcar coming down the drive. Looking out, I see headlights sweep the yard then the slamming of doors.

They don't even bother to knock. The sound of the front door smashing sends me leaping for my side-arm. As I come down the stairs one waits in the hall.

"Just the girlie we want," he sneers. It's the creep who got Lyxa in the alley. He stands at the bottom of the stairs, legs apart, hands on hips. He's got a piece nicked from his ear the size of a dime.

I point my side-arm at his brain and tell him to get lost.

His eyes move to the left and so does my gun. But I'm too late. Someone leaps from the cooking-room doorway, up the stairs and grabs me. He's built like a quarter-back. I kick him in the kneecap. He grabs my ankle. My head smashes against the wall. I hear my side-arm go spinning along the passage. The trawler-man grins and kicks it out the back door. He slams it shut. I twist and kick but it's no good. The ape holding me's too strong. There's another guy standing in the doorway. I recognize a reporter I saw in the square. I'm dragged into the front room and thrown on the couch. I catapult forward and head-butt the newsmag punk in the stomach. He collapses with a grunt. He coughs and vomits on the carpet. The creep gets hold of me and slaps me around the head. I shoot across the room. Stars spin. He comes over and stands with his foot on my chest. I twist over and bounce up. I drop into fighting stance. Then I spin on the ball of my foot and send him a bandol changi fit to bust his ribs. He's still trying to get up when the quarter-back grabs my hair. He forces my head back.

"OK," he hisses. "Tell us what's going on."

"Drop dead." I lunge away. A handful of my hair gets left behind. The creep's got to his feet. He grabs me from behind. He lifts his hand and smashes my face. The reporter steps forward. He's still coughing. "Hey," he says. "This isn't the way to do it, you know..."

The creep tells him to shut up. "Anyway," he says, "comes from Earth, doesn't she?" He twists my arm behind my back. "OK princess, where are your folks? There's a rumour your ma knows more about this new distillery than she's letting on."

I turn my head and spit in his face. He slaps me again.

"Out," I say. "Gone out."

It's about an hour before they give up. The creep slaps me around some more. In the end they decide I must be telling the truth. Either that or they're all sick of what the creep's doing to me.

I tell them a load of lies. If I don't then all hell will

162

be let loose and my family will be the first to get burned. I say the distillery's some kind of experimental vessel commissioned by earth-Zone 6 to study climatic changes on Damos. When they want to know why it's been such a secret I tell them I don't know. Yeah – my folks are on it but so what? I cut the apron strings years ago. They go their way, I go mine.

The creep's pleased I'm hurt. He's got his revenge.

Before they go, they smash the place up. They break the furniture, toss stuff from the cupboards.

They even wreck my skeeter which breaks my heart into a million bits.

One gets a rope and ties me although I don't know where they think I'm going in this state. I take deep breaths, clench my teeth. They fix my hands and feet and take me upstairs. They chuck me on the bed.

"Don't try telling anyone about this," the creep's threatening me through a red haze of pain. "No one'll take your word against ours. Anyone who's got anything to do with the project's not very popular around here."

"You're kidding?" I manage to croak.

"Anyway," he goes on, touching the bruise on his face where I kicked him. "With a bit of luck no one'll find you." He bends over me as he speaks. His breath stinks of Elix. "How does the prospect of starving to death grab you, princess?"

I close my eyes.

I hear them clattering down the stairs. Then the

sound of the groundmotor. Then nothing, only the painful, laboured rasping of my breath.

I can see out my window. The sky is a vault of stars. Ananke and Luna bathe in their midst. There's hardly any aura left around Luna. I remember the legend of her tears.

I can see a great, black cloud hovering on the horizon. I lie, only half-conscious.

My dreams are of sea caves and song.

When I come to the sun is high. My muscles are relaxed and the ropes are loose. On the floor my tikker, still working, says it's three hours to launch.

I twist my body and sit up. I work my hands. My back and shoulders are stiff with bruises. The ropes have rubbed my wrists and ankles raw. I sit still. I breathe deeply. I shut my mind against the pain.

At last one hand's free. Ignoring the blood I wrench the rope off. I untie my feet. I rub the circulation back.

I grab a blanket and hobble downstairs. The place is wrecked. My side-arm lies outside the back door. I bend slowly and pick it up.

The sea's almost up to the gate. It washes around the feather-tree trunks that have been dry since they grew there. I crawl into the ocean. The salt stings my torn scalp and tortures the cuts on my legs and body. On my face I can feel the old wound has opened up. The water feels cool. I rest in the shallows.

When the sea has washed me clean I crawl out. I wrap the blanket around me and draw my knees up

164

to my chin. The west wind blows through my hair and dries it to a frizz.

I stare out to sea.

Then Troy comes across the dunes towards me. He arrives, panting. He crouches down beside me.

"Hey Sab, been swimming? I'm really glad you're here. I thought I'd better let you know there's a huge crowd down by the quay. Skipperjon went off to join them before I could stop him. It's that rally Frog's old man's organizing. They're going to try to hijack some boats to try to sabotage the..." Troy's face falls a million metres when he sees the state I'm in. "Sab?" he whispers. "What's happened to you...?" He touches my cheek gently. "Sab ... for godsake...?"

I crack a stiff grin. "I got a visit from that creep who got Lyxa and his quarter-back sidekick, that's all. They had some guy from the newsmag with them. They said there were rumours about the ship and wanted to know where my ma was."

My voice sounds really weird. As if it's coming from someone else.

Troy makes a noise in his throat, then gets up and starts kicking sand around. "I'm going to get those creeps," he shouts. "Now..."

He starts running off down the beach.

"Troy!" When I call he comes running back. "Troy, I'm OK..."

"Like hell you are!" He sits beside me and holds

me gently against his body. I can feel him shaking with anger.

"Listen," I say, "we've got to get down to the quay, try to stop those guys going out to the ship, they'll only be killed. The authorities will think they know the truth."

I push him away and struggle to my feet.

"Sab ... how could they do this to you?" Troy's voice trembles with fury.

"How could I let them, you mean. Come on, I'll get dressed."

We go slowly indoors. Troy finds some salve and medi-plast for my cuts. I put on my leathers.

"Let me help you."

"No..." I hold out my arm. "I'm OK."

I pull on the last of my jackets. It hurts like hell.

"They smashed my skeeter," I say sadly, picking up one of the bits.

"Oh, Sab..." Troy's voice cracks. His hands are clenched into fists. "I'll kill them, I swear it."

I manage a shrug. "Don't worry. Where we're going it won't be any use anyway."

The Ship

Before we leave I take a last look round. On the floor, amongst the ruins of my father's furniture, is one of Lu's red ribbons. I tie my hair back with it.

"Troy," I say. "We've got to find Ringo and Lyxa – if we're going to carry out our plan we need as many allies as possible."

Troy shakes his head. "No one's seen Lyxa or her family since the carnival."

"They must have gone out to the ship."

"I guess they must."

"Seen Frog?"

"Not since we went to watch the carnival ship take off."

"We'd better find him too."

"He'll be with his father down by the quay. You know Frog – won't want to miss anything."

Ringo's at the library. She's up a ladder, shelving books.

When she sees us come in she looks down. She smiles.

"Sabra, you brought that book back? Mr Bumpa's been on about it. Hey..." She comes down the ladder quick. "What happened to you?" She looks horrified. I guess she's not used to seeing girls with bruises.

"Had an argument with someone."

"I should think you did."

"Ringo." I'm getting impatient. Time's running out. "Come with us, will you?"

"Where to?"

"The quay," Troy pipes up. "There's a rally going on and talk of some of the trawlermen going out to the sh ... er ... to the distillery."

"I shouldn't really leave ... it's not even lunch-time yet."

I touch her arm. "Ringo ... please. It's important..."

Ringo looks at me for a minute. Then she takes her apron off. "OK, Sabra," she says. We go out without a backward glance.

"What's the rally about?" Ringo asks as we make our way to the sea front.

"About the new distillery," I lie. "It's being commissioned today."

Ringo claps her hands together. The light catches the rings on her fingers and they sparkle like ice-diamonds.

"How exciting! Why are the trawlermen going out there? My brother works on one of the boats but he never said anything about. . ."

Troy glances at me. "You'd better tell her," he says.

"Tell me what. . .?"

So in a quiet voice I tell Ringo it's not a distillery at all but a ship that's been built to take the premier and Gummant reps on a long, long sea voyage.

Ringo claps her hands again. "The premier? In Narran! Oh, Sab, will we see him?"

"I doubt it. He's been on board for days, so have the Gummant reps."

"But why did they tell us it was a distillery?" Ringo goes on.

Troy looks at me again. "We'll tell you later," he says. "It's not safe now."

Ringo starts to protest but by now we're heading for the harbour. Along the cobbled street we can see crowds heading the same way. Shop doors are open, street stalls unattended. Ringo runs on ahead and talks to a scared-looking woman pushing a kiddipram in the opposite direction. Then she waits.

"That lady says there's going to be trouble," she

says, looking worried. "Don't you think it best if we keep out of the way?"

I link my arm through hers. "Stick with me, Ringo, we'll be OK, I promise."

In the gutter lies a discarded newsmag. Troy picks it up.

"Looks as if that reporter believed you, Sab."

He hands the newsmag to me.

The story of the research ship's on the front page. A smaller story at the bottom tells of storms and tidal waves in eastern Mainland. Part of the fenland farming areas are under water. In several places the sea wall's been breached.

It's only just beginning.

At the harbour we push through the crowd and stand by the wall. The tide's running high and fast. Waves are coming over the breakwater and the base of the Mermaid statue is submerged.

As we look out to sea a dozen or so trawlerboats head out round Narran Point towards the middle of Selkie Sound. A cheer goes up.

In the crowd a couple of folk are waving banners: "DOWN WITH THE GUMMANT", "PEOPLE ARE MORE IMPORTANT THAN PROFIT". The wind almost whips them from their hands. Then someone comes along and tells them to take the banners down. "The Gummant have fooled the lot of us," he says, showing them the newsmag. "New distillery my foot.

170

We might have guessed. No wonder they wouldn't use local labour."

As copies of the newsmag are passed around the crowd gets more noisy. Then someone hops on the wall and shouts for silence.

"That's Frog's father," Troy whispers in my ear.

Sure enough, Frog's standing at the speaker's feet looking upwards with poppy eyes. His red cap's tilted on the side of his head. As I look, someone knocks it off. Frog scrabbles about under people's legs looking for it. When he stands up he sees us by the wall. He waves and starts to make his way over.

Frog's pa begins to speak. He's rattling on about a Gummant cover-up and how a research ship's been built with Narranese resources but the people are getting nothing out of it.

"Not even a new distillery," he's shouting, "when the old one's needed updating for more than thirty years. We're going to sabotage the commissioning, that'll let the swines know how we feel."

"I didn't think they *wanted* a new distillery," Ringo says in my ear.

"There's no pleasing some people," I tell her.

Troy takes my arm and pulls me away. "Sab, should we tell them now, do you think? While everyone's here? They'll never stop the ship going now so your family will be safe."

But I've seen mobs like this before. I remember the

blood riots on Maja V. The only thing the crowd listened to were the words of laser-rifles.

"What, the mood they're in?" I say. "No Troy, that's not the way to do it. Believe me, I know."

"How then? We planned to tell people as soon as we could, remember?"

I shake my head. "Not like this. If by any chance they believe us, which isn't likely, there'll just be panic. There's got to be some other way."

"How then?"

"Trust me Troy, huh?"

"Sab, we've only got a couple of days. Look at the water, it's higher than I've ever seen it." Troy looks frightened and angry.

"I'm not blind, Troy."

He grips my arm, right where it's bruised. I don't flinch. "Well, you'd better make your mind up quick, Sab," he hisses, "or else I'll do it for you."

He walks away, hands in pockets. I see his grandfather Skipperjon come over and take his arm. Troy's saying something to Skipperjon and I've got a good idea what.

Just then Frog gets to us. "Hello, Sabra," he croaks. "Goodness me, what a turn out. Isn't it exciting? You know it's about time people made their voices heard, my father's been saying it for years. Fancy that project not being a distillery at all, it just shows how you can fool people. Especially when they're as apathetic as this lot. They drink too much Elix that's the trouble . . .

Hey, you been in an accident? You look a bit battered ... where's Troy ... oh there he is with Skipperjon I'll just go over and say 'hi' ... Do listen to my father he's such a good..."

I turn away from him and lean my elbows on the sea wall. Out on the rocks past Narran Point I see dark heads gathering. I look over my shoulder but no one else's noticed. They're all too busy listening to Frog's father croaking on about workers' rights.

Then we hear gunfire and Frog's pa stops ranting and raving and turns. In the distance we see puffs of smoke.

"They've fired on the trawlerboats," someone shouts.

And, sure enough, the boats are turning and heading back to the shore. We wait as they chug around the headland and into the harbour. One's badly damaged, its wheel a smouldering mass of twisted timbers.

The crowd mill about. A section breaks off and runs to take the ropes as the trawlerboats come in alongside the quay. There's a lot of shouting. As one of the captains disembarks a reporter from the newsmag runs towards him. He gets pushed away as the captain heads for the nearest bar. The photographer clicks his camera at a couple of bodies being carried away on stretchers. One's face is covered by a blanket. A woman runs beside it, crying into her apron. There's a smell of scorched timbers.

Then, suddenly, there's silence.

Not even a song comes across the water to break it.

The trawlermen stand motionless at their masts. The crowd draw breath. All together, as if a great wind has come and blown all their protests away.

By my side Ringo clutches my sleeve and points out to sea.

Then all I can hear is the beating of my heart.

I feel a hand on my shoulder and when I turn Troy's there.

I hear Skipperjon's hushed voice. "What the hell is that...?"

But my throat has closed up and no words come.

Accompanied by a flotilla of patrol boats the ship my mother described to me comes sailing through Selkie Sound. Behind her, a clamour of black and white sea-scavs weave and dive, skimming her wake like Fleet-fighters. In all my lifetime I've never seen anything like her. I've seen a hundred different classes of space-cruiser. I've seen fighting ships. The neat, swift Watch-dogs of the Fleet and the great iron war-wagons of Ulta with their indestructible robo-knights. I've even seen a fleet of the legendary golden long-ships plough across the red seas of Mars but, oh boy, I've never seen anything like this.

The vessel glides slowly, hardly disturbing the water. The throb, throb of her engines drums confidently across the waves towards us.

They seem to be sending a message of farewell.

Her wooden hull's broad, deep, rising to a high point at the bow. A figurehead's carved there but I can't suss out what it is. Inside the hull's been built a multi-storey living unit that stretches from bow to stern. Rows of portholes are like the eyes of a mud-worm. Small boats hang on ropes beneath the bottom row. On the top deck a transparent dome houses some kind of vegetation.

I remember my ma telling me the vessel was the best designed lifeboat in the history of history. I guess she was right.

Beside me several folk are looking at the ship through some kind of primitive eye-spy glasses. They gaze, spellbound, at the image in their lens. One guy puts his down, then up again to his eye as if he can't believe what he's seeing. Skipperjon hands his to Troy. Troy gazes through it for a minute then gives it to me.

I scan the decks but there's no one there. Not my ma, nor Pa, nor Lu come out to wave goodbye. I can just make out faces pressed to the portholes taking their last glimpse of dry land for what could be a long, long time.

Two flags fly from the observation platform. The aquamarine and white striped flag of Narran and the multi-starred flag of Mainland. When I move the lens I see the figurehead's a man with a crown topping his long, flowing hair. He's holding a three-pronged fork of some kind.

Then I see a name's been painted on the side. It's a word I don't immediately recognize.

Then I remember tales I've read in my books of old-Earth legends.

They've called her...

NOASARK

Even when the ship's gone out of sight the crowd stays. The flotilla of patrol boats that accompanied her disperse and sail off towards the horizon. Troy's still standing with his arm around my shoulders.

There's a sudden rush of wind as if the whole world has sighed and given up.

"Come on," I say. "Let's go get a drink, huh?"

The crowd are still milling around. They're talking in hushed tones now. Some are shaking their heads in disbelief. Then a small group break away and march off towards the Council rooms. A guy's appeared with a mobile brew stall. He's selling cups of the stuff as if it's going out of fashion. Frog's pa's surrounded by a group of trawlermen. They're waving their arms around telling what happened out there. Frog's pa's shaking his head and saying he doesn't know what else they can do.

"It's gone," he's saying. "They've beaten us." People nod their heads and wander away.

Skipperjon comes with us to the Net and Skimmer. Up the cobbled street people still linger in their doorways. One or two look at me with hostility. I look the same way back at them. Skipperjon asks me where I got my bruises.

"People digging for muck," I tell him.

The old guy shakes his head. "I don't know what this place's coming to. Beating up girls..."

"I'm OK," I say. "Really."

I'm beginning to wonder what all the fuss is about.

As usual I've got no bucks so Troy gets the beer.

"I should get back to work," Ringo says although she still looks a bit stunned by what she's seen.

I glance at my tikker. "Soon be closing time," I tell her.

She sighs and shrugs. "Oh well ... if I get the sack, I get the sack." I'd hate to remind her that in a day or two's time there'll be no library to work in anyway.

Skipperjon sits and stares into his mug of Elix. "I've never seen a vessel like that," he says. "Never in all my years as a seafaring man."

"My mother built the engine," I tell him.

"Yes ... I know." Then he looks at me with his shrewd, boat-builder's eye. "What exactly is it for, Sabra?"

I look at Troy and I know the time has come.

"You'd better tell him," Troy says.

So I do.

When I've finished the old guy shakes his head. "You're having me on, Sabra," he says.

"No, Skipperjon." Troy leans forward and puts his hand on the old man's arm. "She's not, honestly, the whole thing's true."

Ringo and Frog are sitting with their eyes popping out. Frog begins to splutter... "And you mean Lu's on there, oh wow. And what's going to happen to all of us I'd like to know. I suppose being ordinary working folk we don't matter."

And so I tell them exactly what's going to happen to us.

In the corner the juke thumps out a Whizz-kidz song that was a hit on earth when my pa was in primary. It's called "Day of Destruction".

Skipperjon laughs. "And if you expect me to believe *that*, you two, you must think I'm senile."

"I told you, Sab," Troy says. "I told you no one would believe us."

"I believe you," Ringo says.

I give her a hug. "Thanks, Ringo."

Frog gulps as if he's swallowed a buzzer-fly too big for his gullet. "So do I. I've been studying things like that. It's all quite logical and you know Earth is a much more advanced civilization." He swallows again. "I think we should try to think of some way of persuading people to..."

"You're crazy," Skipperjon says. "Half the people on this island are afraid of the Sirens, the other half's afraid of swarks. No one will just walk into the sea. It would be better to..."

"So you *do* believe us," Troy says.

Skipperjon pulls on his weed-pipe. He frowns. "I believe a flood might be coming. I've seen weather signs I've never seen before and I've got to admit it scares me. But the other thing..." He shakes his head. "The best thing we can do is persuade people to evacuate the town. Go up to the Heights ... take whatever stuff they can carry with them."

I shake my head. "It won't do any good, Skipperjon."

The old guy gets up. "Well, Sabra, you can please yourself. I'm going to knock on a few doors. My family have lived on Narran for generations, people will take notice of me. You've been here a few months. Just see who they believe and who they don't. Troy? Coming?"

Troy looks at his grandfather. Then he looks at me. I can see the fight he's having with himself. Then I feel him clutch my hand under the table.

"I'm staying with Sab," he says quietly.

Skipperjon shrugs. As he goes out Troy gets up and runs to him. He says something. The old guy listens. Whatever Troy's saying is making the old guy look thoughtful. Then he frowns and stares at Troy. He slowly nods his head. Troy gives him a hug. He stands in the doorway and watches his grandfather go up the street.

"What did you say to him?" I ask when Troy comes back.

"I reminded him of something."

"What?"

Troy gazes at me. "I reminded him of the time I fell off his boat," Troy says. "I asked him who he thought saved me then."

I crack a grin.

"Oh, dear." Ringo's been silent up to now. She gets up suddenly. "I'm going home. I've got to warn my parents." Then she starts to cry. "Sabra, Troy, I'm so frightened."

I get up and put my arms round her. "Ringo, it's OK. Trust me."

"OK," she sniffs.

"And anyone else you meet, try to persuade them to go to Narran Point. Say there's a meeting or something ... anything ... OK?"

Ringo sniffs again and wipes her eyes. "All right, Sab."

"Go with her, Frog," Troy says.

"Me? I'm going home to tell my folks to get ready. Oh, dear..." Frog goes out still rattling on. I can't help grinning.

Behind the counter the barman's reading a newsmag. "Load of rubbish in the newsmag these days," he says. He takes a swig of Elix. "They couldn't even get the story about that ship right if you ask me. If that was a research vessel I'm a Mainlander. Don't know why everybody buys it." He chucks it in the garbage bin.

"Does *everyone* buy it?" I say to Troy.

Troy shrugs. "Guess so."

The barman's given me an idea. Don't know why I didn't think of it before. I finish my beer and get up.

"Come on, Troy."

"Where to?"

"You'll see."

Outside, the streets are getting back to normal. *NOASARK*'s already yesterday's news.

In the newsmag building the editor's in the front office punching buttons on a typing machine.

When he sees me he looks sheepish.

"Come to make a complaint, Earther?" he asks.

I grin. "Nope. Just a friendly visit." I touch the bruise on my forehead.

In the back there's the reporter. When he sees me and Troy he comes out.

"Look," he starts to say. "I'm really sorry..."

"Are you the creep that...?" Troy goes to grab him. I hold him back.

"Take it easy, Troy. I don't need you to fight my battles."

"But...?"

"I mean it, Troy!"

I'm packing my side-arm so I take it from my belt. Slowly, I spin the chamber and click it shut.

The editor's mouth drops open. So does the reporter's.

"OK," I say. "Get your notepads, I've got a story might interest you."

We go back to the cottage to spend the night.

When I awake and look at my tikker it's three o'clock in the morning. I can hear the waves lapping. Troy's asleep beside me. His arm's thrown across me like he's scared I'll get up and go. I lie quietly, unmoving, listening to the sounds of the sea. The only other noise is Troy's soft breath as he murmurs my name in his sleep.

I think of all that's happened. Leaving Earth. My buddies. I try to make a picture of Skin in my head. It's a job remembering his face. All I can see are bits of him. His eyes. His hands. The jewels in his ears. It's like a picture cut into pieces. I think about the voyage here. The vid-trax where I first saw footage of the Sirens. I remember meeting Troy at the top of Narran Point. How I thought his eyelashes were the longest I'd ever seen. I think about sitting in that sea cave with all the remains of previous habitation scattered about like signposts pointing to something I couldn't see. I think what a great place it will be to live.

Then, suddenly, as if they read my fantasy, the air's full of songs. I hear them echoing wildly above the wind and the waves. I move Troy's arm gently aside and get up.

Outside the foam from the breakers reaches the

back step. I look up and in the sky there's a new star. It seems to get brighter and brighter as I watch.

And then I see the Sirens. There must be a hundred. More.

The music's louder than ever before. It echoes across the mutinous sea towards me. I know they see me standing here.

I know that they are waiting.

Sea Caves and Song

I wake Troy at dawn.

"Time to go," I tell him. I get my old Sunday bear and my book of old-Earth legends. I wrap them carefully to try to protect them from the water. I stuff them into my bag. On the mirror is my sister's ribbon. I put that in too. I put on my leggings and jackets.

"Anything else?" Troy says, looking round.

I shake my head. "Never did believe in lumbering myself with a load of gear."

The water's halfway up the stairs. Amongst the other stuff floating around are bits of my skeeter. Troy picks up a piece with the skull painted on. He gives it to me.

We wade out the back door. The water's nearly to the road.

Even though it's almost day, the sky's filled with night.

Leaning into the wind we walk along the cliff road to the town. Winding its way up to the Heights is a straggling caravan of people. Some push kiddiprams full of household belongings. Others lug suitcases. Women carry stuff on their heads. Their apron pockets bulge. One or two call out to us as we pass, tell us we're heading the wrong way. We ignore them.

In town, one or two shopkeepers are nailing boards to their windows. I want to tell them they're wasting their time. A cartload of sandbags are being unloaded in the square. The tide's up to the Net and Skimmer.

We head for Ringo's place. She's there, sitting on the front doorstep, crying.

"They wouldn't listen to me," she sobs. "Then Skipperjon came round last night and they went off to some meeting. They didn't come back. I waited because I knew you'd come for me, Sabra."

She gets her bag and follows us to Skipperjon's where Troy's stuff is. Someone's been in and looted the place. Furniture's overturned, cupboards rifled. Troy's so angry he almost weeps.

"If you lived on Earth you'd expect nothing else," I tell him.

He gets a picture of his parents who died when he was a kid and his collection of model boats.

"Anything else you want?" I ask him.

"Only you," he says.

"Where're we going now?" Ringo trots to keep up with us.

"To see if Frog's at home," I tell her. "We can't desert him now, can we?"

Ringo sniffs and nods. She wipes her face on her frock.

By now the wind's whipping past us like a speed-flash. The cobblestones are awash. The sky's as black as doom. A copy of the newsmag floats past.

On the front page is the story of the Sirens. They'd dug out a picture of the statue that used to be at the harbour entrance before it got washed away. There's a list of what people should do and where they should go.

It's my guess no one's read it.

Frog's at his place trying to stuff a million things into a school-bag. "Everyone's gone up to the Heights," he says gulping as if he's swallowed a flitter. "My father went out last night and when he came back he said people were talking a load of rubbish and the only place to go was to high ground, but I told them there's no rush, by my estimation it should be at least another eight hours before..."

"Frog, you coming or are you staying here to drown?" Troy helps him stuff his maths books into the pocket of his bag.

"I'm coming, of course." He lugs his bag on to his shoulder and almost falls over.

"Gimme," I say, taking it from him.

"I might never see darling Lu again," I hear him say to Ringo as we climb the cobblestones and make our way to the road that leads to Narran Point.

I turn. "Don't worry, Frog," I say, lightly. "You can't get rid of my sister that easily. I know, I've tried."

"Yes, Sabra," Frog says. "She told me what a bully you are."

A few months ago I'd have thumped him for saying that. Now I just grin.

The town's deserted now. Shutters rattle and the wind whistles through the open doorways of empty buildings. The street's littered with dropped belongings and an atmosphere of terror like the threat of nuclear war. My heart's heavy with regret. Troy sees the look on my face.

"Sab," he says. "We've done all we can."

"Have we?" I say bitterly. The wind takes my words and flings them to eternity. Troy puts his arm across my shoulders.

"You know we have. If you'd stood up in the square and shouted salvation till you were blue in the face no one would have listened."

"They were relying on me to tell people," I say. "And I've let them down."

Troy shakes his head. "No Sab, their songs will be there for everyone to hear. They did before, maybe they will again."

I shrug.

Perhaps he's right.

Halfway up the road we turn to look. Already the harbour's disappeared and mountainous waves are smashing into the town. The trawlerboats have broken their moorings and are tossing around helplessly. As we watch, one smashes against the half-submerged warehouse and breaks into a thousand bits. Ringo's crying softly, clutching on to Frog's hand. He's going on about something but no one can hear what he's saying. Past Lyxa's house we see the windows are shuttered, the gates closed and locked.

"I bet she'd rather have stayed with us," Ringo sobs.

"Yeah." I put my arm round her. "I don't suppose she had any choice, do you?"

Ringo shakes her head.

I think of my ma who didn't have any choice either.

I walk with my head low and, for the first time since coming to Damos, wish I was somewhere else.

I feel Troy's fingers pushing my hair away from my face.

"Sab...? You crying?"

I shake my head. "Who me?" But I don't look at him.

Then his face is close to mine and for a minute we stop. He buries his face in my hair and I feel his body shake.

Then, above the screaming of the wind I hear Ringo shout.

"Sab! Troy! Look...!"

And when I look up my eyes are full of people.

In front of us.

Behind us.

Everywhere.

Some sit in groups. Others stand around. When I turn, more are coming. As we stand and stare they pass us. One or two speak to Troy. Ringo runs to a woman and throws her arms round her. A figure detaches itself from the crowd and comes towards us. It's Skipperjon. He hugs Troy and thumps him on the back. Then he holds out his hand to me.

Troy shakes his head in disbelief. "What...?"

"The newsmag came out last evening," he says. "Special edition." Then he shrugs his shoulders. "There was a meeting in the Council rooms. I reminded everyone of what you said, Troy. How you believed the Siren folk saved you. And if it wasn't them, then who was it? We took a vote at midnight."

"We didn't think anyone would believe us," I tell him.

"We can't deny our history, Sabra, and if my boy tells me something then I believe him. Us old 'uns remember the folk tales passed down to us by our parents, our grandparents. We remember stories of the old religion even though, somewhere along the line, we'd forgotten why our ancestors worshipped the goddess Sirena. They had forgotten what happened to Troy until I reminded them." The old man shrugs his shoulders. "Some of us have been up to the Heights. Most of the wildlife's gone. Up to the forests on the slopes of the volcano we reckon. It'd take weeks to hack our way through." He wipes his eyes where the wind's bringing tears. "Some have stayed up there to take their chances but we're willing to follow you if you'll show us what to do."

Troy whoops with triumph and jumps around. He hugs me, almost lifts me off my feet. Ringo's crying again. This time with happiness.

And the joy in my heart's like a Siren song.

A hour or so later it seems as if the whole town's here. I stand alone at the top of the steps and see the water only a metre below. Through the gloom of the storm's afternoon I strain my eyes.

But the sea's empty.

"Sab!" I hear Troy call. He's sitting with a bunch of people, cross-legged round a wind-blown fire. Sparks shoot upwards like celebrations. In the blue-black sky Ananke's clearly visible. So's Luna. Her aura's gone, disappeared. Her tears have fallen to earth. Hiding behind the horizon's thunderclouds the golden god Chrysos awaits his new bride.

When I go to sit beside him, Troy says, "Tell them what happened when you fell off ROCKENROLLER."

So I do.

As I'm speaking others gather round. They ask me questions and I tell them all I know. Then I tell them some of the legends of old-Earth. Stories I've read in my ancient books. I get one out of my bag and it's passed around. I tell them to be careful, it's about a thousand years old.

It's as dark as midnight when the first of my beloved Sirens comes. I'm sitting at the edge of the cliff with Troy, watching the wind-whipped sea. I take his hand and hold it to my mouth.

On his skin I taste the ocean.

The first thing I see is her head above the waves. I can't suss out why she isn't singing. Then I realize, it's the one from the carnival. She holds up her arms in silent greeting.

Then, suddenly, the air is full of music. And as the Sirens sing the wind dies down and the sea becomes a smooth, smooth mirror as dark as wine. Their music's filled with promises.

My heart is filled with peace.

My mind with visions of sea caves and song.

There must be hundreds, more than all my wildest dreams foretold. They swim and dive like fairy creatures. Their tails-flick in the moons' glow turns the waters to silver and to gold.

I turn to call the others. But they're already here. Ringo's beside us. So's Skipperjon and Frog. Frog's croaking on about something but his voice is drowned in song. The others crowd silently behind us.

Troy looks at me and grins.

We reach out our arms together.

Read Point Fantasy and escape into the
realms of the imagination; the kingdoms
of mortal and immortal elements. Lose
yourself in the world of the dragon and
the dark lord, the princess and the mage;
a world where magic rules and the forces
of evil are ever poised to attack . . .

Available now:

Doom Sword
Peter Beere
Adam discovers the Doom Sword and has to
face a perilous quest . . .

Brog The Stoop
Joe Boyle
Can Brog restore the Source of Light to
Drabwurld?

The "Renegades" series:
Book 1: Healer's Quest
Book 2: Fire Wars
Book 3: The Return of the Wizard
Jessica Palmer
Journey with Zelia and Ares as they combine
their magical powers to battle against evil and
restore order to their land . . .

Point

Pointing the way forward

More compelling reading from top authors.

Flight 116 is Down
Forbidden
Unforgettable
Caroline B. Cooney

Someone Else's Baby
Geraldine Kaye

Hostilities
Caroline Macdonald

I Carried You On Eagles' Wings
Sue Mayfield

Seventeenth Summer
K.M. Peyton

The Highest Form of Killing
Son of Pete Flude
Malcolm Rose

Secret Lives
William Taylor

Point Romance

If you like Point Horror, you'll love Point Romance!

Are you burning with passion and aching with desire? Then these are the books for you! Point Romance brings you passion, romance, heartache, . . . and *love*.

Available now:

First Comes Love:
To Have and to Hold
For Better, For Worse
In Sickness and in Health
Till Death Do Us Part
Last Summer, First Love:
A Time to Love
Goodbye to Love
Jennifer Baker

A Winter Love Story
Jane Claypool Miner

Two Weeks in Paradise
Spotlight on Love
Denise Colby

Saturday Night
Last Dance
New Year's Eve
Summer Nights
Caroline B. Cooney

Cradle Snatcher
Kiss Me, Stupid
Alison Creaghan

Summer Dreams, Winter Love
Mary Francis Shura

The Last Great Summer
Carol Stanley

Lifeguards:
Summer's Promise
Summer's End
Todd Strasser

Crazy About You
French Kiss
Robyn Turner

Look out for:

Two-Timer
Lorna Read

Hopelessly Devoted
Amber Vane

Russian Nights
Robyn Turner